MR DARCY'S ABDUCTED BRIDE

JULIE COOPER

Quills & Quartos
PUBLISHING

This is a work of fiction. Names, characters, businesses, places, events, locales, and incidents are either the products of the author's imagination or used in a fictitious manner. Any resemblance to actual persons, living or dead, or actual events is purely coincidental.

Edited by Jan Ashton and Katie Jackson

Cover by Susan Adriani, CloudCat Design

ISBN 978-1-963213-05-8 (ebook) and 978-1-963213-06-5 (paperback)

To our sweet and lovely Katie, daughter of my heart

CHAPTER 1

Mrs Bennet despised her houseguest. To be sure, there was not much to like about him, unless one took seriously his compliments to her fine table, which she accepted as her due. Even in these, however, he had an air of rehearsed puffery; he would doubtless just as enthusiastically apply his accolades to Lady Lucas's table, which was mean in comparison.

Fleetingly, she felt a trace of guilt for her resolve that Elizabeth *must* marry him, regardless.

Quickly, however, she quashed it. Had *she* loved Thomas Bennet, ten years older than herself and not nearly so handsome as the least of her suitors? No, she had not. Sensibly, her own mother had, by means neither gentle nor affectionate, drawn her seventeen-year-old daughter's attention to the advantages of the match, the size of the home she would inevitably rule, and the degree to which her future children would be elevated. It was for those unknown, unborn offspring that she had sacrificed her girlhood fancies; now was the opportunity for one of them to keep the dream alive, to preserve the Longbourn estate unto her grandchildren.

To this end, she had overcome her inclination to put Mr William Collins in the third-storey spare room usually occupied by draughts and damp; as well, she stifled her hopes that he might not too heartily anticipate his future occupation of her home. Instead, she had begrudgingly prepared for him her nicest guest chambers—a suite of rooms across from Mr Bennet's. Elizabeth was unlikely to be a comfortable bride; it was important that he not be overeager to look elsewhere.

Surely she will not look this gift horse in the mouth, Mrs Bennet reassured herself. Instead of a bleak, impoverished life as a spinster, she would gain a lovely residence in Kent in the present and become mistress of her girlhood home in the future.

Still, a conversation overheard the previous evening had unnerved her.

Mr Bennet had been unable to attend her sister Philips's dinner party due to his latest health complaint—which was nothing unusual, for he hated dinner parties as much as he loved his illnesses. Elizabeth, in relating to him of the evening's events afterwards, had used the time to complain of that awful Mr Darcy's past treatment of Mr Wickham. Had there been something of passion, perhaps, in her long and detailed recital of Wickham's injuries? Could she be developing a *tendre* for the handsome lieutenant? There was no future in it!

Naturally, Mrs Bennet found nothing wrong with a bit of *flirtation*. At the age of one-and-forty, a longing for the youth and beauty of her past almost tempted her to flirt with the fine-looking man herself. But *passion* was tantalising, and it would be even more difficult for Elizabeth to see the advantages of connexion to the odious Mr Collins with passion's cloying tentacles gripping her heart. Her daughter had recounted the lieutenant's pitiful tales until Mrs Bennet had been forced to interrupt with complaints of her own—which, predictably, caused Mr Bennet to begin whingeing again about *his* sufferings, effectively turning Lizzy's attention back to himself.

Naturally, the girl had been all solicitousness then, full of consideration towards her father's latest ailment; she always gave *his* grumblings far more consideration than her mother's. The complaint was not a serious one; Mr Bennet's infirmities never were, and Mrs Bennet half expected that he employed them in order to keep the attention of his family—*especially* Elizabeth—upon himself, and to exacerbate her own nerves with the ever-present reminder that he held only life tenancy in his own estate. Still, it was also true that he would not easily part with his favoured daughter, much less to a man the two both enjoyed ridiculing.

A marriage to Mr Collins is in her *best interests,* she thought with renewed resolution. Could her husband so blatantly ignore Lizzy's future? Surely, he wanted the best for his favourite.

Yet, a niggling discomfort reminded her of how easily he ignored so many things, herself most of all. The workings of his mind remained ever-baffling.

The arrival of Mrs Hill interrupted her muddled thoughts. "Mrs Bennet, Mr Jones has come to see the master. I took him up."

"Thank you, Hill," she mumbled, still distracted by her chaotic contemplations.

"You are so very welcome," the older lady answered cheerfully, quickly departing and leaving Mrs Bennet with raised brows. It was another mystery. Hill had been in an exceedingly jolly mood of late, with a spring in her step and a jaunty disposition unnatural to her. It was disconcerting, and Mrs Bennet had worries enough.

Sighing, she took herself to her husband's chambers to learn the latest diagnosis for such ailments as he pretended to possess.

"I have made him a special tonic. He is to have a dose twice daily, without exception. It will cleanse his corrupted intestine while strengthening his heart."

"Why not calomel?" Mrs Bennet asked. Whatever his verdict on the source and cause of any affliction, Mr Jones *always* prescribed calomel.

"This situation requires a more serious treatment."

Mr Bennet glanced at her, a definite note of triumph in his gaze. '*You see, my complaint is serious,*' his look said. '*I told you so.*'

Fear filled her breast. She was accustomed to taking lightly his agitations, just as he took hers. That he should be *truly* unwell was terrifying! That her future should be so gravely at risk, was unbearable.

Mr Jones measured a dosage from a large bottle and administered it to his patient. Unlike the calomel—which did nothing much that she could tell except make the chamber-pot an immediate necessity—a beatific smile shortly thereafter emerged in place of Mr Bennet's usual smirk.

"Darling," he said to his wife, taking her hand and tugging her closer. "Come sit with me."

She frowned.

"My work is done here," Mr Jones announced. "My joints tell me that the rain on the horizon shall be our first true winter storm, and I wish to be home 'ere it arrives. Call for me if he worsens."

It was two hours before Mrs Bennet could extract herself from her husband's chambers. Whatever was in that medicine put her husband in an excessively *friendly* mood, and not at all as if he were lying at death's door. Yet she could not ignore the apothecary's words; it was more important than ever that the repulsive Mr Collins be chained to the welfare of her family by the bonds of matrimony.

As if she had summoned him, Collins's oily voice rang out from the open door of his sitting room. After a very few moments of eavesdropping, she understood them to be a rehearsal of a marriage proposal! To have happened upon him, and it, at this particular moment was divine sanction, and she could not overlook it; nor, however, could she overlook his choice of wording, with its liberal stream of blunders. Lizzy would not appreciate any of it, and Mr Bennet, in his current state of inebriety, would be of no help in forcing her to think past the inconvenience of a stupid husband and towards the rewards of a life of security and ease. In fact, forcing Lizzy to do much of anything was easier said than done.

There was no hope for it: she *must* delay this proposal until her husband was well, if she did nothing else.

"My dear Cousin Jane...no, no, no, Cousin *Elizabeth*. Elizabeth. Elizabeth," Mr Collins mumbled, repeating her name a few more times before continuing. "Almost as soon as I entered my future home, I singled you out as the companion of my life. I am run away by my feelings—"

Boldly she rapped on the door jamb.

When he saw his visitor, Mr Collins's unctuous smile creased his face; he was not at all embarrassed, it seemed, at the possibility he had been overheard. His next words proved it.

"Ah, how opportune your visit! I was only gathering

my thoughts in preparation for a forthcoming event we both, if I may so delicately deduce, anticipate. May I hope, Madam, for your approval when I solicit the honour of a private audience with your fair daughter, Jane—pardon, not Jane—with *Elizabeth*, this morning?"

This morning! So soon! Even knowing that the marriage was for the best possible motive, no female would appreciate so little an attempt at wooing. How stupid was he?

Incredibly so, it appeared. And Mr Bennet was in no condition to provide any sort of reinforcement—if he even would! Frantically, she searched her mind for any possible means of delaying.

Her mind, for once, complied.

"Oh dear! Yes—certainly. I am sure Lizzy will be very happy—I am sure she can have no objection. One little request, just a small thing, surely, but meaning a great deal to the bride. This one ambition has been the greatest desire of her heart since a child. She has always wished, nay, *longed*, to be married out of the common way. By a licence, that is."

She saw the shocked look upon his face, and hurried to continue before he could voice his objections.

"Of course, her dreams are not *only* romantic. Just think—once a fellow and his lady have decided to wed, why wait three long weeks for the banns to be called, when he can make her his own the very next day?"

She saw the moment the idiot realised, by the lascivious expression crossing his face, that he would have a female in his bed at least three weeks sooner by this method; she gagged a little at the idea of it. Resolutely, however, she pressed her advantage.

"Now, a smart man would go to town and procure the licence before he says anything at all to his bride."

His brow furrowed. "He would? Why?"

Yes, Fanny, why? Think! "Because…because what woman could resist an offer revealing that her suitor has paid such attention to her desires as to have *already* procured it! What affections for that man shall be stirred within her breast at his consideration!"

"Hmm. Perhaps so. However, might she also, and rightly, despise the extravagance of this gesture, and feel instead that a husband who avoids such spendthrift ways is a superior choice of mate? Besides, surely Cousin Jane—er, rather, Elizabeth—would be flattered at receiving so good an offer, as to make such deeds unnecessary?"

Unsurprisingly, he was a tight-fisted miser who believed the gift of his ample person to be ample reward for any female lucky enough to earn his attention. It was a temptation to knock him over the head, bury his body in a shallow grave, and hope that the next in line to inherit was someone even slightly worthier. God would surely understand. But she forced herself to think past the impulse, speaking instead to his parsimonious soul.

"Oh, but of course I would never expect *you* to finance this romantic scheme. Your sacrifice of time and effort in order to fulfil Lizzy's dreams is sufficient contribution. I will naturally provide you with adequate funds to compensate you for the expenses of the trip… Shall we say, twenty pounds?"

She did not suppose he could accomplish the whole thing in one day. If she were truly fortunate, Mr Jones's predicted storms would delay him further—*if* she could just send him on his way before the bad weather arrived. But even counting fare to London and back, a night or two at an inn, and a bond to secure the licence, twenty pounds was far more than was necessary. As she had guessed, his small eyes alit with greed; his obstinacy gave way before his avarice.

"I suppose it is the right thing to do, indulging my bride in her dreams," Mr Collins opined. "I am a generous man always, I hope, and she should not be made to wonder whether her husband will do all that is necessary to increase her happiness. Still, perhaps I ought to speak to her first, so that she might experience the pleasures of anticipation."

"No!" Mrs Bennet's protest was far louder than she had meant, and he reared back in alarm. She moderated her tone. "It is just that the *surprise* is everything to her. It will ruin all if you reveal the gift before she is allowed to open the package, so to speak."

Reluctantly, and after a few more arguments, he agreed. She sent Hattie to help him pack for his journey, and then set about the tedious task of writing a letter of permission for the underage Elizabeth's marriage, and then the even more tedious task of having Mr Bennet sign it without enquiry as to what it was for. Fortunately, his medication precluded all sensible thought, but it required considerable amorous effort instead and so, while thus engaged, she wheedled the twenty pounds from him, which saved her the further exertion of searching his book-room. All told, it was a successful, albeit exhausting, morning. She had gained herself at least a day and maybe three for her husband's recovery; certainly, he would force Elizabeth's agreement—and possibly by then, Mr Collins might even have memorised her name.

All five of the Bennet sisters displayed varying degrees of surprise when Mr Collins announced his departure for London in the early afternoon.

"Oh, but do you intend to miss the ball?" Lydia exclaimed.

"Perhaps our cousin does not find such amusements proper, and has no intention of accepting Mr Bingley's invitation," Elizabeth offered smilingly.

At this, Mr Collins turned to her. "I am by no means of such an opinion. I assure you that I am so far from objecting to dancing myself, that I shall take this opportunity of soliciting your hand, Cousin Elizabeth, for the two first dances especially—a preference which I trust my cousin Jane will attribute to the right cause, and not to any disrespect for her."

Mrs Bennet watched with chagrin as Elizabeth's face fell at this open sign of his preference for her, and the distaste with which she accepted. It was disheartening to see, and all her earlier relief at achieving a brief delay plummeted. How was she to ensure the girl accepted his crucial offer of marriage?

CHAPTER 2

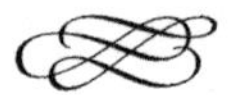

Five days later

Mrs Bennet slumped against the wall just beyond Mr Collins's door. After returning from the ball at Netherfield far too late, and attending to Mr Bennet's all-too-frequent requests for companionship far too early, she departed his bedchamber only to hear, once again, the sonorous tones of Mr Collins's marriage proposal rehearsal coming from his sitting room.

Yes, Mr Collins had returned from London, but no—she had made absolutely no inroads into bettering Lizzy's opinion of him. It had been all she could do to convince him to wait until after the ball to propose.

Nor had his lovemaking undergone any substantial improvement in his absence. He now seemed to remember to whom he proposed, but that was the best she could say for it. The rest was a long, tedious recitation of his reasons for marrying and the bride's good fortune that he was willing to marry *her*. There was nothing at all in it of *his* good fortune in gaining a wife so much prettier and more intelligent than himself.

Mr Jones had declared that he did not see enough improvement in Mr Bennet's health, and the medication continued—despite Mrs Bennet's opinion of her husband's vigour. The odds of Lizzy accepting the vicar's proposal without her father's help in forcing the issue were slim.

Cursing Collins silently for waking so early after so late a night, when sensible folks ought to remain in their beds until noon, she could think of nothing more useful than locking the odious vicar into his room and pretending the door was stuck, when a momentous idea occurred to her.

Its sudden appearance in her fatigued brain must surely signal more divine approval: *Mr Bennet's tonic.*

Its medicinal properties resulted in, um, *congenial* effects towards those of another sex. It might not work upon females as it did for males; neither had she any idea whether it would work as well upon a fellow whom one despised. She had not observed Mr Bennet's attentions straying to the maids, so it did not render one mindless—Lizzy might still recognise Mr Collins and all of her former opinions of his desirability. Unless of course...she increased, perhaps even doubled or tripled the dosage? But how could she arrange for Lizzy to ingest it?

Another heavenly sanction—in the form of a remembered favourite—imbued her with an idea: Hill's candied ginger syrup. Its strength was enough to disguise any unusual flavour, and she always kept some on hand, as it was useful in elevating simple desserts into works of art in the case of unexpected company. Elizabeth was excessively fond of it, and if it was sugared well, and served with the currant pudding Cook had prepared as a masterpiece for tonight's table, and if Mrs Bennet ensured that Lizzy consumed every bite...well, it would have to do. Afterwards, she would arrange for an audience with Mr Collins; Lizzy would, in her newly amenable state, agree to the marriage, and Mrs Bennet would hurry the couple to Mr Palmer with the precious licence in hand, and see them wed before noon today!

"Hill!" she screeched, hurrying towards the kitchen to bully Cook into surrendering her pudding. "Hill! I need you at once!"

The ball had been an utter failure. If not for Jane's triumph—two sets with Mr Bingley, one of which was the supper dance with his escort and full attention thereafter —it would have been a complete waste of a new dress. But Elizabeth laughed to herself at the drama in these sentiments, for a new dress was never wasted, and had it not been for her fury at the callous Mr Darcy's pride in his hideous treatment of Mr Wickham, the lieutenant's absence from all festivities, and the ruin of her shoe roses in that first set with the clumsy Mr Collins, she would have said the evening had been highly entertaining. She had danced nearly every set, and though her partners—with the notable exception of Mr Darcy—were unremarkable, the food, decorations, music, and company had been excellent. Whatever one wished to say about Miss Bingley's character, she hosted an excellent party.

Avoiding Mr Collins thereafter had been problematic, and overhearing his bold addresses to Mr Darcy—giving that gentleman yet another reason to look down upon the first family of Longbourn village—excruciating. Why did her cousin single her out for his attention? If he thought to *woo* her in the future—and she sincerely hoped it was not so—she would have to ensure she was away visiting the Gardiners upon his next visit. At least she had not had to bear with his irksome company for the four days preceding the ball. Though he had made much of the mystery behind his reasons for leaving, she believed he had meant to be gone only a day or so. The succession of rain which had inundated the valley from the advent of his departure until the morning of the ball had, evidently, delayed his journey both going and coming, with the result of his return arrival at Longbourn barely in time to dress for the event. His conversation during their dance consisted of a long litany of complaints of mud—horses who could not walk in it, coachmen who could not navigate it, and clothing ruined by it. Had she not been certain of her innocence in all matters pertaining to his absence, she would have been convinced that he blamed *her* for the whole of his troubles! She would have to relate the tale to Papa for his enjoyment.

Poor Papa! His illness had begun to unnerve her. While his appearance and appetite seemed as usual, he could seldom finish a conversation without dozing off, and stranger still, for the most part he wished only for Mama's company. Papa had been in no state to attend a ball, and she could only hope that he soon would recover, as he had so often in the past. After breakfast, she would insist upon spending the morning at his bedside, whether or not he slept, and hope she could notice some improvement to his condition.

A glance in the mirror told her that she was well enough in appearance, although she had not bothered with putting her hair up and her dress was a simple, ancient one that she could don herself. They would have no visitors this morning, and Elizabeth would be surprised if her younger sisters—who had spent far too much time at the punch bowl last evening—would arise before afternoon tea. She had taken two steps towards the door, when it opened, revealing her mother with a tray.

"I did not understand, I swear I did not understand her intent, not until too late!" Mrs Hill muttered anxiously to herself. Mrs Bennet, of course, had never meant her to understand anything at all; however, the mistress was much too accustomed to gabbling aloud most every thought in her head, had much too little experience with devious plotting, and most often forgot her servants had functioning ears.

Guilt ate at her; Miss Elizabeth was the sweetest, smartest girl imaginable, and her mother was *drugging* her —drugging her so that she would accept that foolish Mr Collins as her husband.

Yet...what right do I have to interfere? There is no question but what an excellent match it would be for her—possibly her only opportunity for any marriage, any future at all.

Such was Hill's agony of indecision, that she almost missed the sight of the man standing in the shadows just beyond the hermitage—she, who prided herself on missing nothing! How long had he been there? Why was he here in broad daylight?

It did not matter; the important thing was that she had *not* missed him. Mr Harwood *was* here. Such a wise and sensible person as himself would surely help her think of a means of preventing the catastrophe on the horizon. Glancing around to ensure she was not being observed by anyone, she slipped from the house.

Fitzwilliam Darcy had made up his mind. When Bingley departed for town today, he would go as well; to that end, he informed his man, Harwood, of the change in plan. Harwood could ride in his carriage with his trunks while he rode with Bingley. He would spend the journey helping

Bingley to understand that pursuit of a connexion to Jane Bennet was the worst possible idea. There was nothing wrong, *per se,* with the girl, except that her mother was pulling the strings of her life, and he could not abide her pulling Bingley's as well.

Well, perhaps one other thing was wrong. Her sister, Elizabeth Bennet.

He could not bear it, now that he understood Miss Elizabeth bore feelings for his enemy. Her defence of Wickham had been vehement and eager—there was no mistaking yet another young lady fallen beneath the rogue's spell. He had tried to warn her, but to no effect; the ladies never saw what was so plain to him, the thin and shallow nature of Wickham's veneer of respectability.

You did not see it either, for a much longer period, Darcy reminded himself. *Not until it was far too late to undo the damage, and* you *knew him for years.*

He shoved the reminders and the guilt from his mind. He must get out, now, before he threw away his own familial pride and bound himself to a bride from a family utterly lacking in propriety and affluence. While Miss Bennet and Miss Elizabeth were both respectable and decorous, their younger sisters were allowed to run wild—and did so. Their cousin Collins—his aunt's ridiculous parson, he had been somehow unsurprised to learn—was *heir* of their Longbourn estate—a fact the man had, in Mr Bennet's absence, flaunted amongst the populace.

Never mind that Elizabeth possessed a haunting sort of loveliness, a mixture of sweetness and lively spirits, with her wide, dimpled smile that he yearned to kiss into; a lithe figure he was dying to hold close; and a mind full of wit, conversation, and sparkle that he could not help engaging at every possible opportunity. If she were near, he would never be unhappy again a day in his life.

Stop it, Darcy! It was precisely this sort of unrealistic thinking that kept him awake at night, a victim of her siren-song. He wanted her. He could not have her. Better to flee instead. But his thoughts whirled round and round, teasing him with memories.

Harwood entered at long last, with the news he had waited for.

"Mr Bingley is ready to leave, sir," he said.

"Excellent. I shall join him directly."

Harwood nodded but remained unmoving. Inwardly, Darcy groaned. Harwood was the ideal gentleman's gentleman. He stayed informed—and made sure Darcy was, as well—with the state and intricacies of any household they inhabited; his taste was impeccable, he was never unprepared or forgetful, and he anticipated Darcy's needs with a prescience that seemed almost uncanny. All this, he performed with a sort of understated elegance of manner, never aggressive, gossipy, or obtrusive. In the absence of orders otherwise, he usually slipped away immediately. When he did not, it meant there was news, and none that he was likely wishing to hear.

"If you would be so kind as to lend a moment of your time," Harwood murmured, in that way he had, his manner somehow making any refusal impossibly coarse.

"It has to do with events at Longbourn this morning," he said.

"Why should I care for any of that?" Darcy snapped, appalled by his sudden desire to hear every possible detail regarding the situation, no matter how insignificant.

His man looked at him, just looked, and he realised what he ought to have predicted—Harwood *knew*. He understood, without Darcy ever mentioning a thing, that his employer was obsessed with the second eldest daughter of Mr Thomas Bennet.

"What has happened?" he asked, his tone surly. He turned away to rearrange the items upon the chest of drawers nearest him, since he could disguise neither eagerness nor resentment from Harwood's all-seeing eyes.

"It appears that Miss Elizabeth Bennet will receive a proposal of marriage this morning, if she has not already."

"Marriage? To whom?" He struggled to sound nonchalant.

"Mr William Collins, sir."

His heartbeat, which had begun a frantic, pulsing rhythm, smoothed again. "What of it? She would never agree to yoke herself to such a fool."

He could not say how he knew this; he simply did. Not for three estates the size of Netherfield would she give herself to such a nincompoop.

"Reportedly, and unbeknownst to her anticipated bridegroom, she has been drugged, sir. The concoction she has received is of a nature that, my source is convinced, creates a docile, even an, er, overly affectionate response in its object."

Darcy spun to face Harwood, horrified. "Would not Collins realise that his wished-for bride is intoxicated? No, no, no, do not answer that question. But I cannot believe her father would condone such an act!"

"Her father is currently in no condition to understand what is happening in his household, or to prevent it if he did."

Darcy had known the man was ill, but he must be out of his head to be unaware of such an affair.

"My informant believes the young lady will be taken to the church this morning, and there be wed to Collins. There is already, evidently, a licence. I have observed the vicar, Mr Palmer. He is elderly, obtuse, and hard of hearing. I do not think Palmer would comprehend the situation, were the girl to topple over during the ceremony."

He did not question the source of Harwood's information. If his man believed it, it was undoubtedly reliable. Of course, none of it was legal, but what good would the law do when Elizabeth's reputation and character were already ruined? Nor did he waste time attempting to think of someone else who might attempt a rescue. He knew of no one in this entire county who was able to act decisively. Probably, most folks would believe—even knowing the situation—that it was unfortunate, but all for the best in the long run. Sir William Lucas would doubtless gleefully disseminate the news as joyfully as if Elizabeth had been wed to a duke.

Elizabeth! No! Dearest, loveliest Elizabeth must not ever be sacrificed on the altar of self-interest and impure motive. Fortunately, he was already dressed for riding out.

"Inform Mr Bingley I will be unable to travel with him after all. Tell Frost to have Bingley's best hunter saddled for me, and have my brougham brought round and ride with him to Longbourn. If you meet the Bennet coach along the way, have Frost contrive to block its passage. It would be best if she is never even put into the carriage, and we can halt this nonsense before there are more witnesses to its execution."

Harwood nodded once, slipping from the room as quietly as he had first entered it—plainly satisfied with his interference.

Who works for whom? Darcy wondered.

CHAPTER 3

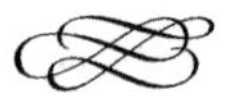

"Mama." Elizabeth was tilting alarmingly to one side on the settee, her eyes nearly crossed. "I want to find my bed now, I think."

Mrs Bennet understood her daughter perfectly, despite the fact that she dropped approximately a third of her syllables. Mr Collins, too busy composing the next sentences to his foolish, drawn-out offer of marriage, failed utterly to comprehend.

"What was that? What did she say?"

It was the fifth time he had asked it. One would think he would pay more attention to the utterances of the recipient of his protracted proposal—but one would be as wrong as it was possible to be. She felt, again, a heavy measure of guilt for inflicting him upon Lizzy. But what else was there to do? Their prospects were a fathomless unknown, beholden to this very fool!

Without Mr Bennet to provide support for the

marriage, she had about as much chance of convincing Elizabeth to marry the idiotic Collins as she did of persuading her husband to buy a house in Mayfair. Lizzy was her most intelligent daughter, yet the girl was frustrating in her inability to secure her own future!

"She says she cannot wait to be wed, she thinks," Mrs Bennet interpreted.

Mr Collins's brow furrowed as he seemed to notice, for the first time, that his hoped-for bride was listing to one side. "I say. She seems to be a bit off this morning, does she not?"

Her daughter went off into a fit of giggles. Mrs Bennet was required to hold her phial of salts beneath Lizzy's nose, to transform it to a fit of sneezing instead.

"It is not every day that a young lady receives a marriage proposal from a handsome, eligible gentleman," Mrs Bennet reminded him, once the sneezing was past. "It is unsurprising that she is nervous."

His brow smoothed. "Oh. Why yes, believe me, my dear Miss Elizabeth, that your modesty, so far from doing you any disservice, rather adds to your other perfections."

Elizabeth's voice dropped several notches—and in unfortunately clear tones, began quoting one of Mr Bennet's favourites. "'But pain is perfect misery, the worst of evils, and excessive, overturns all patience.'"

"I have always loved Shakespeare," Mr Collins opined, smiling approvingly at Elizabeth. "Not long ago, a very notable lady—my esteemed patroness, you know—particularly advised and recommended that I commit Shakespeare's sonnets to memory whilst in the pursuit of a bride, and I cannot help but believe that your knowledge of his works, especially when tempered with the silence and respect that her rank will inevitably excite—will ensure her approval of my choice of bride. I compliment you."

Even Mrs Bennet knew—not through any interest of her own, of course, but from the endless ruminations of her husband—that it was Milton which Lizzy quoted, not Shakespeare. She wondered whether, within all these words Mr Collins had thus far uttered, she could presume an actual proposal of marriage had already taken place. If so, she could proceed with Lizzy's response.

Unfortunately, in the absence of any question, there seemed no space to provide an answer.

"My reasons for marrying are, first, I think it is a right thing for every clergyman in easy circumstance..."

Heavens above, would he never bring himself to the point?

"Mama, the sound of his voice is making me sick," Elizabeth mumbled.

Mr Collins stopped his monologue on the excellence of Lady Catherine de Bourgh and looked again to Mrs Bennet for interpretation.

"She says she has always wanted to marry a cleric."

He smiled benignly, and began another soliloquy upon the subject of Elizabeth's lack of fortune and his own generosity in ignoring it. "And now nothing remains for me but to assure you in the most animated language of the violence of my affection. I deem it appropriate to declaim using Shakespeare's poetry such as young ladies are prone to admire, in demonstration of my regard." He cleared his throat and began to recite:

> Take all my loves, my love, yea, take them all.
> What hast thou then more than thou hadst
> before—

It was at this juncture that Mrs Bennet noticed Mary standing in the entrance to the parlour, very near her own chair, looking on in some amazement. Mr Collins continued with his performance, oblivious to anyone else's presence—including his intended bride's.

"What is he doing, Mama?" Mary whispered.

"Have you no sense of romance? Have you never before heard poetry recited?" Mrs Bennet hissed.

"Really? But why would he choose Shakespeare's verses about a friend's betrayal with his own mistress?"

"Hush, noisy girl! Your father and sisters are abed. Out!"

Mary, fortunately, obediently departed, but if Jane waked, she would not be so easily put off. It was all too much, and Lizzy was in danger of collapsing.

"Mr Collins!" she called loudly, interrupting some lines which did, unfortunately, sound much as though he were scolding a disloyal friend and deceitful lover.

He peered at her in some irritation. "I have three more stanzas learnt."

"But you have missed my dear Elizabeth's bestowal of her hand and heart upon you. And now, in her excitement to be your bride, she wishes to be taken to the church immediately and have the thing done."

"I did? She will? She does?" he asked, staring at his bride-to-be. Elizabeth had laid her head upon the arm of the settee and was laughing to herself, glassy-eyed.

"Can you not tell excitement for a wedding when you see it? We shall use the carriage. I have already ordered it brought round. Mr Palmer will have witnesses available. Do you have the licence?"

"Why yes. Yes, I do. Right here in my pocket." He fumbled around with three different pockets before finally producing it. He glanced at Elizabeth again, and this time there was no mistaking the gleam of admiration in his eye as he realised he was to be a married man before noon.

Forcibly quelling her conscience once more, Mrs Bennet heaved her daughter to her feet. "Come, my poppet," she said, keeping her arm about Lizzy's waist. "It is time to be wed. Your future is secured."

Darcy galloped up the long drive just as a party of three emerged from the house. One of them was obviously the hulking form of the cleric, Collins. His jaw could be seen flapping, a never-ending stream of discourse reaching Darcy as a tuneless whine. Mrs Bennet walked by his side, plainly and heavily supporting Elizabeth. Even from this distance he could see the poor girl would probably collapse onto the pavers, were someone not holding her up. He could hardly believe his eyes; the plan to ruin Elizabeth's life depended upon a scheming mama, a witless groom, and a doddering vicar—and yet, it appeared to be proceeding apace.

He managed to manoeuvre his mount between the group and the carriage before they reached it, leaping from the horse to land practically upon their toes.

"Mr Darcy!" Collins beamed at him with his usual vapidity, bowing low. "You honour us with your presence. In fact, it was the only thing lacking on an otherwise perfect morning. I do not believe that I presume too much when I and my cousin invite you to join us on a brief journey to the village church, to thereby witness our nuptials. The distinction of having so fine a testator would be a compliment to myself and my bride, and I do not hesitate to add, nearly as great a commemoration as the presence of Lady Catherine de Bourgh herself."

"I am certain it *is* an impertinence to ask," Mrs Bennet snapped, appearing more impatient than guilty. "Pray forgive him for his insolence, sir. As you can see, we are just departing. We will be on our way, and trouble you no further, Mr Darcy."

Elizabeth giggled.

"Miss Elizabeth," he said in firm tones, ignoring the other two, "can you understand that you are being taken to a church to be married to this man?"

At the sound of his voice, she looked at him and smiled

her wide, lovely smile. "You are very pretty," she said in the too-careful tones of the inebriated. Reaching over, she touched his mouth. "It is such a shame you are vermin. Scoundrel. Rat. Ch-churl." She peered up above his head, as if searching for more invective in the sky, swaying a little. "Brute. Mig-headed piscreant. No, that was not right. Never mind." She shook her head, causing another sway that her mother only just prevented turning into a tumble.

Mrs Bennet was sweating now with the effort of keeping her daughter upright.

"Toad," Elizabeth pronounced carefully.

"Miss Elizabeth!" Collins screeched in horrified tones. "I assure you, Mr Darcy, she means none of it! Perhaps in her excitement for her wedding—"

"Lizzy, come with me, now!" Mrs Bennet pulled her daughter to the side, attempting to get around him. "Mr Collins, forget this nonsense and help her into the carriage!"

"Miss Elizabeth is going nowhere with the two of you," he said, stepping in front of the pair of women, effectively blocking their path forwards. "Anyone can see she is not in her right mind."

"Simply because she does not care for you—and had the courage to say so to your face—does not render her irrational. I daresay women have been lying to you for a chance at your fortune for years," Mrs Bennet snapped, clearly furious.

Elizabeth was searching the sky again. Taking another

step forwards, Darcy firmly tugged her away from Mrs Bennet's hold, placing his hands on either side of her face so that she was forced to look directly at him.

"Do you understand that your mother is attempting to force you into a marriage with your cousin, Mr William Collins?"

As she gazed into his eyes, her own beautiful dark ones filled with tears. "You were unkind," she whispered, and though her speech was not pristine, and she tripped over some of the syllables, he understood well enough what she said next. "Why not...simply say...in no mood to dance?" A single tear spilled over, and he slid his thumb across it, his heart aching. How he wished he had never attended that stupid assembly! But she was not finished tearing his integrity to shreds. "I love to dance," she sighed, still swaying to an invisible rhythm, still peering up at the clouds. "Dance with the...clumsy. The ugly. The awkward. No matter. To twirl, to whirl. Freedom, for an hour. But you..." Her eyes rested again directly upon him. "You ensured I knew I...no better than something scraped off your shoe. You, sir, are no mentalgem. Genmaltem."

"Gentleman," he said, helping her. He forgot their audience, and even his purpose in being there, only wishing he could feel the delicate skin of her cheeks through his gloves, longing to kiss away those tears. "I am sorry," he said softly. "I have regretted those words many times. You are correct. I am a brute."

"Mr Darcy," came a somewhat frantic cry from Collins. "I apologise if my cousin, in a moment of forgetfulness, neglected to demonstrate all the respect due your consequence. I beg your forgiveness and can assure you that, as her husband, I will ensure such insolence never occurs again." He cleared his throat and drew his bulky form up even taller. "Miss Elizabeth, I order you to proceed at once to the carriage. You may regard my instruction as a command."

Darcy gave him a sour look, but the interruption did remind him of his purpose. "Miss Elizabeth is plainly out of her senses. Taking her to a church in this condition, with intent to wed, is not simply illegal, it is immoral. It is depraved."

"There is nothing the matter with her that a wedding, with its accompanying joy, would not resolve. This is none of your affair, Mr Darcy," Mrs Bennet retorted.

"Now, now," Collins reproached, "we none of us wish to cause offence in so illustrious and honourable a person as the nephew of Lady Catherine de Bourgh. He simply misunderstands the situation. Mr Darcy, Miss Elizabeth has given me her assurances that she wishes for the marriage to take place. I have a licence! A licence!"

To Darcy's amazement, he extracted a piece of paper from his pocket and fluttered it before them both like a banner, continuing his chatter.

"Possibly you mistake my bride's liveliness and high spirits for conduct instigated by less flattering motives. However, I can reassure you that nothing such as you imagine is the source of her behaviour. Once she is my wife, I shall assist in refining her comportment to match that exhibited in the higher circles which I have the good fortune to inhabit regularly, and which, naturally, she shall wish to emulate."

"I do not criticise *her*, you dolt," Darcy snapped. "How can you not see that she is out of her head? Miss Elizabeth," he said, more sternly this time, desperate to direct her attention to the offence in progress. "Do you understand that your mother is trying to wed you to this buffoon, right now, at this very moment?"

Instead of answering, Elizabeth laid her head on his shoulder. "I am very sleepy."

Both Collins and Mrs Bennet made their moves—Mrs Bennet attempting to pull her daughter back, Collins trying to shove her away from Mr Darcy and gasping at her effrontery in touching the 'great man'—but Darcy blocked them both. At that moment, his carriage thankfully turned up the drive. It was plain to him that the only recourse was to carry Elizabeth away from these reprobates until she was in her right mind. If he had to drive all the way to London and back to gain time enough for her to regain her sensibilities, that was what he ought to do.

"Miss Elizabeth," Darcy asked, "shall I take you for a drive in my carriage?"

She smiled at him. It was answer enough.

"Come," he said, and lifting her in his arms, strode to meet his oncoming brougham, which stopped beside them several yards away; one of Bingley's stablemen sprang out to put down the step. As he helped her into the carriage, Darcy glanced back. Collins's mouth was an 'o' of surprise, while Mrs Bennet, her fists clenched and very red in the face, called for him to bring her back this instant. Ignoring them both, he climbed in after Elizabeth, leaving the stableman to return Bingley's hunter. Settling himself, he knocked on the roof. Moments later, they were off, Elizabeth curled up beside him, a contented smile upon her face.

The situation was, of course, absurd, ridiculous, even offensive.

How was it, then, that it struck him as so oddly right, so impossibly perfect that she be exactly where she was?

"I do not understand," Mr Collins said, still gaping like a fish. "What has happened?"

Mrs Bennet looked at him with some contempt. During the entire interlude, he had done naught but accuse Lizzy of misbehaviour. Obviously, he worshipped at the altar of the aristocracy and made excuses for every insult. How Mr Darcy had learnt of the morning's scheme, she could not guess; perhaps it was coincidence. Probably it was. He was departing Netherfield, or so it appeared, and likely come to pay his respects—only to have that fool Mr Collins announce his immediate marriage to Lizzy who acted, to anyone with eyes to see, completely soused. Mr Darcy was arrogant, but hardly stupid.

On the other hand, Mr Collins was the most credulous fellow she had ever had the misfortune to meet. Nevertheless, he had influence, of a sort—with Mr Darcy's aunt, no less. Perhaps something could be salvaged of the situation. She may have failed to gain the heir of Longbourn estate for Lizzy, but perhaps a marriage was still possible. Mr Darcy might be no worthier, but he was certainly wealthier, more intelligent, and better looking than Mr Collins. She turned to face him.

"What has happened, my dear Mr Collins, is this: Mr Darcy has eloped with your bride."

CHAPTER 4

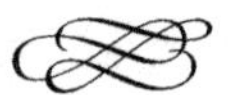

Elizabeth wakened gradually, feeling as if she was drifting within a pleasant fog. The first hint she received of something strange afoot was the sound of horses' hooves blended with the vibrations of carriage wheels rolling upon cobblestone pavers. She must be dreaming, she concluded, a very vivid dream. Perhaps she travelled to Wales; she had always wanted to see it. She had no sooner reached this conclusion when she realised that, rather than the comfort of a seat cushion beneath the weight of her body, she felt something much different. It took her several moments to realise what it was, however; in her foggy state, deducing that she was being held within strong arms, that firm muscles and expensive wool surrounded her, seemed as fantastic as any dream. Opening her eyes required an effort, and at first, everything appeared fuzzily out of focus. Gradually, however, she was able to discern shapes, and finally details.

It began with a chin. That it was a male chin was undeniable—firm, cleft, with a shadow of beard just beginning to show. A thin scar cut through the perfection of its form, running from that chin until it disappeared into the twists and coils of the exquisitely tied cravat framing it. It was a familiar chin, somehow, and yet not Papa's; as well, neither Papa nor his man would ever expend so much effort on such a knot. Her gaze travelled to his hair, a bit overlong and barely brushing his collar, curling at its ends in just such a non-conformity as to exasperate any good valet. The urge to touch it seemed a natural one; she found it as soft as it appeared.

Her touch moved to the bristled chin, held suddenly still, motionless as a deer once startled. Her vision had not deceived her as to the hardness of its shape. A stubborn chin, she decided. A chin which knew the direction it faced, and was unafraid to travel it. The jaw supporting it was a worthy accessory, squared, determined, unwavering, perhaps even descending into dogged. She reached up farther, to the lips set above it. They ought to be soft, gentle, and tender, to restrain that chin and jaw's effect upon the whole. Gleefully tracing them with her fingertips, she realised they were everything lips ought to be.

It was absurdly difficult to lift herself so that she could explore further; thankfully, the strong arms supporting her helped, else she would have had lips and chin only, and how foolish a partial face would that be? With his assistance, however, she could now see the nose—a patrician nose, noble, even. A nose perfectly matching that chin and jawline. A nose of which, undoubtedly, his aristocratic ancestors had pridefully bequeathed to their progeny, an inheritance equally as valuable as castles, forests, and fields. She traced its aquiline shape up to an equally princely brow. The sable brows were soft; the eyes beneath shut, shielded from her explorations.

This was unacceptable. His eyes must be revealed to her. Her mouth opened, her voice emerging only as a whisper.

"Your eyes...they cannot be anything faded, mild, or meek. They must be dark, mysterious, resilient enough to hold the weight of a thousand acres. A thousand tenants. A thousand homes. A thousand mouths to feed. A thousand hearts to break."

At her charge, his eyes opened to her. They could not have been more perfectly set within his features. So shadowed, they were almost black, a fathomless regard that could have sent soldiers to their willing deaths. They were the eyes of command, of duty, of domination. They stared into her soul, seeing too much, stripping her bare. Uncomfortable eyes, and yet, somehow, she knew no other eyes would ever measure up to them in her own sight, again. Sighing, she returned her gaze to his mouth.

"Your saving grace," she said softly, touching once more his lips. "A woman could forgive much, for this."

He was a dream, a fantasy, a man like no other. He would not capitulate to feelings, to emotion; he was much too accustomed to ill winds, stormy seas, citadel-sized obstacles in his path. In that moment, she knew that if she wanted him, she must seize him herself; he would not surrender to simple need or desire. She was inexperienced, yes; but she had power in her, untapped, and he was an admirable foe. If he thought her yet an impediment to his decisive direction, unworthy, easily dismissed, she would show him the error of his ways—and she smiled at the thought. Carefully, she set her lips to his.

In the hour or so since Elizabeth had fallen asleep in his arms, Darcy had conceived a plan—or at least, an objective. The moment she wakened, he must carefully explain to her the situation, ask her where it would be best and safest to deliver her, and get himself away as quickly as possible. He was in the worst of circumstances—with an unchaperoned young lady of good birth. He had considered taking her to the home of her aunt Philips—but that was her mother's sister, and possibly she was not to be trusted. He knew of no other relations except those somewhere in Cheapside. Her friend, Miss Lucas, would probably take her in happily enough, but Sir William was an unmitigated gossip, and instinctively he knew Elizabeth would hate anyone else knowing what had happened. Besides, whether he had her alone in his carriage for twenty minutes or twenty hours, the Sir Williams of this world always drew their own conclusions and told them to anyone who would listen. Avoiding the Lucases seemed best. For lack of a better idea, he continued on towards town; he could always turn a different direction, or even bring her home to Longbourn again once she was fully recovered.

Yet, there were further problems. He did not worry about Harwood or Frost; they would never say a word. He had given Bingley's stableman a large gratuity which hopefully ensured his silence, although one could never be completely certain. Still, it was Mrs Bennet and Collins who were the real unknowns in this situation. Mrs Bennet had shown herself to be ruthless and amoral; Collins was certainly governed by neither intelligence nor common sense. Darcy could, he was certain, have his aunt shut Collins's mouth, but how to shut Mrs Bennet's was, in a word, a pickle. The best strategy on his own part was to rid himself of Elizabeth as soon as he could manage it; the Mrs Bennets of this world could not touch him. But might Elizabeth pay a price, regardless?

He should not care, he told himself. This was not a situation of his own making. He had been avoiding the dropped handkerchiefs—and other, less obvious schemes—of managing mamas and manoeuvring misses for years. He had done what he could, *would* do what he *could* for her, but nothing more.

Then she opened her eyes, those lovely, trusting eyes.

Reaching up, she touched his lips, his nose, his brow. He was paralysed, frozen, helpless beneath those featherweight touches.

Move away, he ordered himself. *Move* her *away. Put her on the opposite bench, as you ought to have done immediately, instead of worrying she might tumble to the floor. Do not be a fool.*

He nearly obeyed that reasoned, sensible voice...that is, until she smiled at him, a slow smile, a dawn's sunlight lighting the horizon, bringing his every sense into the sharpest focus. Until she returned her fingertips to his lips, murmuring words he could not understand.

Until her lips touched his, and he lost his mind.

Darcy was a man who held his passions rigidly in control, always. He had lived in the shadow of a man, nearly his own age, who delighted in freeing them, exorcising them, using them and being used by them. He had seen the destruction in the lives of those wrecked by it. He had spent years attempting to undo its effects, trying, usually futilely, to sort through the ruins for survivors.

One touch of her mouth to his and *he* was the one wrecked, ruined, destroyed. One touch of her mouth to his and he simply...forgot.

His hand slid up her back, up the slim strength of her spine, up into the dense locks of her hair falling over them both, then shaping around her head, holding her to him close and closer still. Her mouth opened beneath his, sweetly, plunging them both into a new country of feelings, a wild hinterland, begging to be explored.

He forgot duty.

He forgot discretion.

There was only Elizabeth, water to a thirsting man lost in a desert so long, he had forgotten its revitalising flavour, the taste of it, its quenching power. In the history of the world, he was certain, there had never been such a kiss. She was Niagara Falls to his parched and drab life, and he could not drink deeply enough. He wanted to drown in her.

"Elizabeth," he said, in what he feared was a moan. "Elizabeth."

His mouth came back down to hers, but she reared back and looked at him, *really* looked, with shocked and startled eyes. She scrambled off his lap, except her limbs did not quite move properly and she fell—or would have done, had he not caught her. Still, she lunged for the door.

"Elizabeth!" he cried, trying to stop her from throwing herself again towards it. "We are moving, drat it! You will be hurt!"

"You do not understand," she panted, struggling. "Out! I must get out!"

Sunshine gleamed in from the window since he had not bothered to pull the blinds, and at last he noticed what he ought to have seen at once—her skin had turned unnaturally pale. He pounded on the roof of the carriage and immediately felt the slowing of its motion. Not waiting for aid from without—or, even, the carriage to come to a complete halt—he half-leapt from the vehicle, hauling her away from it as quickly as possible. Seeing that they were on a deserted portion of the road surrounded only by fields, he set her down beside some shrubbery growing along a low stone wall. They made it only just in time, as she dropped to her knees and retched.

At first, Elizabeth could only shudder with the spasms. She could not stop the audience to her painful humiliation, not when he gathered her hair back and held it away from her so she could cast up her accounts without interference.

Why, oh why was she here in the middle of nowhere, wretchedly ill, before none other than *Mr Darcy?*

He said nothing, but she could feel the heavy weight of his autocratic stare, as if she was the one at fault for this entire bizarre *not*-a-dream state of affairs.

Was she the one? Had she truly been kissing him? Had he been kissing her? Surely not!

As soon as her stomach seemed to have ceased its upheaval, she made a motion to stand. Unfortunately, her limbs were trembling, clumsy, and disobedient. What should have been a nimble move was a general lurching towards the ground, which he only just managed to avert so that she narrowly avoided falling upon her face. It was excessively lowering, when she had already believed she could descend no lower.

"Perhaps you would excuse the imposition of proximity, and remain where you are until your balance resumes?" he asked in his usual haughty tones. "You are not feeling quite the thing, I daresay."

Sarcasm! What she wanted to do was demand explanations, censuring him for familiarity and possibly her abduction. What emerged from her mouth was... ridiculous.

"Ditzwilliam Farcy," she mumbled. "No. Argh." She slapped her palm to her forehead and nearly knocked herself to the ground again.

The act did not prevent her seeing the corner of his mouth tip up, causing an unexpected dimple to appear. "I have been called worse," he said. That almost-smile softened the supercilious air usually attending him; at the same time, it reminded her of the...dream. It had surely been a dream, had it not? It could not be real. No one kissed like that, except in foolish dreams.

Suddenly, she wanted to weep, and only the remnants of her tattered pride prevented her from bursting into tears.

Instead of anything sensible, anything at all, she heard herself semi-incoherently plead three words: "H-help me sit." She wasn't sure whether she had managed to voice even that, but as if he understood her regardless, Mr Darcy picked her up and gently set her on a shaded portion of the wall some distance from where she had... lost her composure. As he moved away from her, she nearly fell over backwards; with one swift motion he settled down beside her, a strong arm around her shoulders, supporting her.

One nod of his head to his men—both stationed beside the coach, pretending to notice nothing—brought a skin of water to her. Carefully he held it to her lips; she took small sips until at last she could no longer taste the strange metallic flavour upon her tongue.

"What... the matter w'me?" She heard the slur in her question, and wondered at it.

"You have been drugged," he said, as complacently as he might have commented upon the weather.

"Wha-what?" The single word she had managed did not begin to express the horror and fear she felt at this revelation. She struggled to move away from him, nearly tumbling off the wall in the process.

Gently, he plucked her back, tucking her into his side. She strained to move away, albeit futilely, until he caught her hands in his own.

"Not by me, *mon rêve*. To the best of my understanding, you must blame your mother. Evidently, she very much wished you to wed your cousin Collins, and administered to you some medication of your father's in order to render you more agreeable to the idea. I think she overdid it."

Mama? Truly? How could it be so? It must be impossible! And yet, a memory struck her, of her mother's arrival in her bedroom this morning, carrying a breakfast tray. Had she not noted how unusual Mama's determination that she eat all of the rather unusually spiced breakfast provided to her? Since when did Mrs Bennet ever *carry* breakfast to any of her daughters? Her excuse of worrying over Elizabeth's exertions at the ball made no sense, in retrospect. It *had* been odd; she *ought* to have been suspicious. She had simply never dreamt that her mother would stoop to such an action.

"H-how...did you..."

"How did my intervention come about? One of your servants informed one of my servants of the plot, and he informed me, only just in time to prevent it. I apologise that there was no opportunity to procure proper chaperonage. Neither did I wish to inform any others, believing you would rather it be kept private."

"I...yes."

She had believed she could be humbled no further, but knowing now that he had been required, by his gentlemanly honour, to save her from an ignominiously plotted marriage to her cousin was the last straw. A tear fell, and then another. She felt them trickle down her cheeks and had neither the strength nor the will to stop them. Every vulgar belief he doubtless held about her family had been proved correct, and she prayed fiercely that if only she could at this moment be struck by lightning, she would never ask God for another thing.

Unfortunately, the sky remained clear, the weather mild. Another debilitating wave of dizziness swept through her, adding to her misery.

"I am sorry," she whispered. There was nothing else she could say.

CHAPTER 5

Her silent tears slayed him. If it were within Darcy's power to knock Mrs Bennet's head into Collins's and pound some sense into them both, he would do it. How could they have so easily dismissed her feelings, her choices, her *health*? Finding his handkerchief, he placed it upon her lap. She took it without a word. Though still supporting her with his arm, he had not felt so helpless, so useless, since his sister's melancholy over her failed romance.

Harwood, however, had never in his life been thus afflicted. He chose that moment to approach.

"Miss," he said quietly, holding out an open tin, "perhaps you would have a peppermint? It settles the belly, it does, and sweetens the tongue."

She looked up then, and Darcy watched as she visibly took command of herself. With a still-trembling hand she selected one, thanking his man graciously, and placing it delicately in her mouth. The mouth he had plundered as if it were pirate's treasure spilled upon a desert isle. Guilt assailed him.

Harwood retreated, and he knew he must as well. In her presence, he was out of his depth; he could not trust himself.

"Where can I take you?" he asked lowly. "My carriage is yours to command."

Turning to face him, her expression was startled, as if he had said something remarkable. But her voice, when she spoke, was calmer now, more…herself.

"Where are we? I have no idea, I fear."

"Frost," he called. "How far are we from London?"

"A bit over half-way."

"London," she whispered. She turned to him. "Can you bring me to my uncle's house? On Gracechurch Street, in Cheapside."

She sounded more assured, as if the thought of these relations gave her strength. It was none of his business; he was duty-bound to carry her wherever she wished. However, if he recalled correctly, was this not her mother's brother? Could the man, a merchant, be trusted?

"If you are certain of a welcome," he said warily, "then of course."

"I am." She took a deep breath. "I think I can walk now."

Darcy realised that his arm was still about her; she was, undoubtedly, wishing for distance. He removed it, grateful that she was more composed but regretting the loss. He stood, holding out his hand to her. She bit her lip. Was she reluctant to take it, to re-enter the carriage with him? Did she no longer trust him?

"If I fall upon my face, do catch me, will you?" She smiled at him, a little crookedly, and the relief he felt was beyond anything. He smiled back.

"Word of honour," he murmured.

Taking his proffered hand, she allowed him to ease her up. He gave her his arm, and together they walked back to the carriage; she trembled a little, he noticed. She was not so steady as she pretended. He handed her in, and then seated himself opposite. Even though their knees were nearly touching, she seemed much too far away. He longed for her nearness, to hold her once again.

For several minutes after the coach was underway, they were silent. As for himself, he did not know what to say. Did she remember what had happened between them? If he apologised, would it only embarrass her? And then—most importantly—the question now constantly circling his brain: Should he offer for her?

The idea did not fill him with the alarm he had once supposed it might. Yes, he would have some work to do in order to compensate an absent settlement, but he was prospering; there was no reason to believe his children would go hungry or Pemberley would suffer, whether or not he married a woman of wealth. Was not a woman of Elizabeth's beauty and spirit worth a thousand fortunes?

And yet…there *was* her family to consider.

At last night's ball, Miss Lydia and Miss Catherine had

made numerous trips to the punch bowl, their flirtatious laughter growing ever louder as the evening wore on, their behaviour towards the officers outrageously appalling. In an obviously hungry bid for attention, Miss Mary had displayed her 'talent' at the pianoforte, without interruption, for far too long—seemingly unaware that she ought to surrender the instrument to anyone else. The idea of introducing *any* of those younger girls to Lord and Lady Matlock was off-putting. Elizabeth's elder sister had almost completely entrapped Bingley; after Sir William's words of anticipation regarding a wedding between them, he had carefully observed Miss Bennet. Her manner, like Elizabeth's, was in every way proper, but there was absolutely no sign of especial attachment. For all he knew, this was yet another, albeit subtler, scheme of Mrs Bennet's, to foist her daughter upon a hapless young man while encouraging the entire community's expectations.

But there were worse considerations—namely, Elizabeth's words spoken in defence of Wickham. Was she taken with the scoundrel? She did not, could not truly know him; it was not within her power to discover his practised deceptions. Ought he to explain something of his past association with the man? Everything within him rebelled at the idea of even speaking his name, bringing him into what had thus far been one of the oddest and yet *rightest* mornings of his life.

Unfortunately, Wickham was already here, a poisonous echo of their history—almost a physical presence in the carriage. So numerous were his reflections, so lost was he within them, that he nearly startled when she spoke.

"Please, tell me the truth, sir," she said, head bent, her voice low and serious. "Did I…did I brazenly attack you?"

He leant forwards, not nearly as close as he wanted to be, but closing some of the distance between them.

"Miss Elizabeth," he said.

She would not look at him, so he gently lifted her chin with one finger. "I knew you were not yourself. I ought to have stopped you. I could have, and yet…the truth is, I forgot myself. You are, to me…" Darcy floundered, searching for words adequately describing his infatuation, his affection. "I had not known you a week before I regretted the poor first impression I gave of myself. You are surely the handsomest woman I know."

Her mouth opened, her eyes widening. "That is not possible. Please, sir, you need not invent flattery. I understand I was not…I was not well. I wish to apologise for what happened, and promise that you need never worry that any word will ever escape this carriage. My uncle and aunt are most trustworthy. If you could only see your way to forgetting this entire day, you would have my sincerest appreciation."

"How I could possibly forget the best few minutes of the last year is beyond me," he said a little drily, remembering those sweet, scorching kisses.

He meant it in acknowledgement of their mutually thwarted passion; she *must* know what she had done to him, what she did to him even now, sitting so near, her lips still swollen from his kisses returned so passionately by her own, her hair in wild disarray from the way he had mussed it within his desire.

But her expression turned to dismay. "You would not... surely you would not go to all the trouble to rescue me, only to see me ruined? If anyone were to hear—"

He sat up straight. "You cannot believe I would do that," he said, much offended.

"I hope you would not."

She sounded doubtful. How could she distrust him? He had changed all of his plans and practically thrown himself at her feet in effecting this rescue! She ought to be looking at him with admiration, gratitude even. Did she believe he would make love to *anyone* he was alone with? There was a man she knew who would, but it was not him.

The ugly spectre of Wickham's influence forced itself again to the forefront of his mind. Was she, even now, wishing that *he* had been her rescuer, her knight in shining armour? *Hah!* If Wickham found himself alone like this with her, he would not hesitate to seduce her. If seduction did not achieve the result he coveted—and even though she was a young lady of good birth—he might, probably *would* take what was not offered freely, and blame her for all of it.

Elizabeth had kissed *him*, first! Yes, he had not thrown her off, but he had hardly pressed his advantage, either. A cold feeling crept down his spine, chilling him. In her dazed state, had she been imagining another? Had it been

Wickham's eyes she had seen, when she looked into his? Wickham's mouth to which she had wished to join her lips? A tiny voice in his brain urged him to say nothing more, but frustration, repressed desire, pride, and...yes, hurt, all combined to silence it.

"My mother was the daughter of an earl. My father's family has owned a goodly portion of Derbyshire for over a century and a half. *Your* mother drugged you and nearly handed you over to your moronic cousin! Which of us, I wonder, could be thought most trustworthy?"

"That is certainly a self-righteous stance you take," she snapped, "considering the unjust and ungenerous part you acted in *your* friendship with another."

He had been correct. Wickham lived in her mind and heart.

"You refer to Mr Wickham, I suppose," he spat. "You take an eager interest in that man's affairs."

"Who that knows what his misfortunes have been, can help feeling an interest in him?"

"His misfortunes! Yes, his misfortunes have been great, indeed!" Jealousy, thick, ugly and venomous shot through him. "Let me give you one piece of advice, to take or discard at your leisure. Do not ever pay *him* such attentions as you so generously bequeathed me, lest you find yourself bearing the consequences of it alone—he would never do the honourable thing, even did you hold a pistol to his head!"

"And you call yourself honourable?" she asked, her voice rising, her eyes narrowing.

"Yes, I do," he said, struggling to put just the right insouciance into his tone, so that she might not know how much the words he uttered now meant to him. "I have been contemplating offering you marriage, after all, for the sake of a few careless kisses."

She sat up straighter, and her eyes sparked with fury. "Well, let me ease your sanctimonious conscience," she all but hissed in fuming contempt. "I would not marry you if you were the last man in England! I had to be *drugged* in order to accept your attentions! May your conceit, your selfish disdain for the feelings of others rise up to choke you!"

Her words sliced through him, inflicting pain with every syllable. In the distress of it, his dignity, his very sense of self rebelled; how dare she, possessing near relations of such tremendous inferiority as to be nearly unmentionable, pretend that his attentions meant *nothing*?

"Oh, it will not, for *my* pride is under perfect regulation. Of what have *you* to be critical? If you are in the mood for meting out judgment, why not complain of the total want of propriety possessed by your younger sisters? They certainly could use a lesson or two upon sobriety."

She flushed but did not remain silent. "My sisters are none of your concern!"

Again, a part of his mind began flailing, cautioning him to cease and desist. Unfortunately, the wild way he wanted her had not diminished; her now obvious disdain only drove him further into a despairing sort of rage. He managed a sneer.

"Miss Lydia, Miss Catherine, Miss Mary, yes—their behaviour is beneath my notice. Your eldest, however, has attracted the attention of my dearest friend. With unscrupulous apathy, she has allowed your manipulative mother to move him as a pawn in her scheming. I bow to her mastery. If it is Wickham you wish to ensnare, I highly recommend your sister's technique—Miss Bennet pretends to desire nothing of her victim, an appealing indifference he would find irresistible. If lessons are to be taught, perhaps she ought to dispense them. You might find her sort of Machiavellian purity to be rather instructive."

Her jaw dropped. Suddenly, to his amazement, once more she dove for the door of the carriage.

Outrage, pure and simple, filled him as he grabbed her to keep her from throwing herself out of it, while she struggled violently against his hold. "What is *wrong* with you? This carriage is moving! Would you bash your head against the pavement in defence of your absent lover?"

As if in answer to his question, she suddenly stilled. For a moment, she simply looked at him. Carefully she straightened; somehow, during their struggle, she had become perched upon his knees, his hands clutching her shoulders. Her chin lifted.

"Unhand me," she commanded, her voice low and firm. "You need not worry that I shall risk so much as a scrape, much less my head, over *any* man." Tears glistened in her eyes, but somehow he knew that she would never allow them to fall. Not before him.

His anger deflated, his rage defeated. What he wanted to do was enfold her in his arms. He wanted to beg her forgiveness with every fibre of his being. The steely expression upon her face told him his desires were useless. Practically one finger at a time, he forced himself to release his hold.

She lifted herself from his lap onto the seat opposite.

"You, sir, are an idiot," she said.

"Yes," he agreed, scrubbing his face with his hands.

Momentary surprise flashed across her features.

There must be an apology she would accept, and he needed to come up with it quickly. At least some of his history with Wickham had to be explained. He must make her understand, somehow, why the man was so vicious, so untrustworthy. Above all, he could not allow their brief association to end like this. As if she truly *had* cursed him, words rose up in a flood, choking him with their panicked incoherence.

And then as he watched, her eyes fluttered shut and she pitched forwards, collapsing in a graceful heap at his feet.

CHAPTER 6

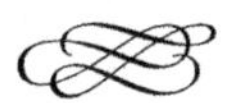

Elizabeth woke to darkness. Disoriented, confused, she sat up quickly and immediately regretted it, rather more gently easing herself back down upon the pillows and shutting her eyes again. Her head pounded with the rhythm of her heartbeat, drumming pain into her body. Was she at home, back to Longbourn?

And why had she wondered if she were *back* to Longbourn? Had she left? Where to? How long had she been gone? Why? For some unknown reason, she felt panic at the question and forcibly quelled the line of examination.

It does not matter at this moment, she told herself. *All that is required at present is one breath in, one breath out. In. Out.* When she felt sufficiently calm, she carefully opened her eyes.

The darkness, she saw, was not absolute. A screen had been carefully positioned by the fireplace to prevent the light from shining directly on her, but the fire was built up enough for the glow to be visible. The air was warm. Cautiously, she smoothed her hands across the linens surrounding her; they were fine ones. She lay upon the softest of mattresses, perhaps more than one. Gingerly, she turned her head to try and take note of her surroundings.

She was not alone. A young woman, probably a servant, sat on a chair by her bedside, chin upon her chest, dozing. On a bedside table, a pitcher was near at hand; at the sight of it, Elizabeth became aware of tremendous thirst. An inch at a time, she eased herself up, but some rustling of her covers must have alerted the sleeping servant.

"Oh, miss! Ye be awake!"

"Water, please," Elizabeth tried to say, but her voice emerged as only a husky rasp. Nevertheless, the girl understood, and poured a cup.

Never had any water tasted so refreshing as this did. She drained the glass, and might have asked for more, had her need for information not been so acute.

"Who are you?" she croaked.

"Molly, miss."

"Where am I, Molly?" she asked, pleased when her voice emerged a bit more strongly.

"At the Golden Fleece, miss," the girl said.

An inn, then, but the name meant nothing to Elizabeth. "Where is the Golden Fleece?"

"Past Barnet, not so far as Whetstone," Molly replied.

It took a moment for Elizabeth to associate the names,

but of course she had travelled to her London relations numerous times, and the towns named were along the main road. Had she been on her way to visit the Gardiners? A carriage accident, perhaps?

The servant stood. "The doctor's been and gone, but now that ye be awake, he'll be coming again, I suppose. Such a to-do as ye caused us! Such commotion in the place as he stirred up, I was like to be getting a pain in the noggin myself. I's to be fetching ye a tray once ye wakened, himself said."

"Himself? Who is 'himself'? Mr Gardiner?" Although making a tremendous fuss was the last thing she would ever expect of her placid uncle.

"I don't know of no Gardiner. Ye came with your pot 'n pan. Mr Buskers gave him nothing but the best of what we have, and the Fleece has enough for the Regent himself, I always say."

"My pot and pan?" Elizabeth rasped, utterly confused.

"You know. Your pot 'n pan, your man. Your husband. Mr Darcy. Ye must've hit your noggin but hard. Who could forget *him*?" She bustled out of the room.

"My what? Who?" Elizabeth tried to cry out, but Molly did not turn back.

Husband? Husband! Mr Darcy? The room spun sickeningly as she tried to rise, forcing her back down upon the pillows. She made herself take deep breaths, until gradually the dizziness eased.

Think, Elizabeth, think. You must remember!

The past replayed disjointedly in her memories, a

magic lantern show with the slides tilting madly or missing altogether. Her mother's voice, saying, 'Come my poppet, it is time to be wed'; Mr Darcy's, telling her in commanding tones that she was being taken to a church to be married. For some reason, Mr Collins was present, blathering on and on. Had he been the one to perform the ceremony?

Strangest of all was the memory of a kiss.

She had been kissed twice before. Once was by John Lucas when they were both twelve, more in the nature of an experiment with a friend. It had been interesting, but not particularly appealing, especially after they both burst into laughter afterwards. The other had been Reginald Goulding at an assembly a couple of years prior; five years her senior, she had thought him exciting for that reason alone, and he pursued her after imbibing a bit too heartily at the punch bowl. It had been reckless, to be sure, and her feelings had been bruised, but not shattered, when he had quite determinedly ignored her ever afterwards.

Nevertheless, there had been nothing in her entire life like the kisses she had experienced within these fragmented memories.

They could *not* have been a dream, for she could never have dreamt such an experience, could never have imagined it. Even now, her body livened at the recollection.

It was *Mr Darcy* who had kissed her, she was certain of it. Had he *married* her? How could she possibly have agreed to marry a man for whom respect was lacking, a man she was not even certain could behave as a gentleman? Yet, she remembered those kisses. She had wanted them, desired them, and, even weak and bewildered, wanted more. She wanted them still. They were not stolen moments nor fleeting, friendly experiments; they were neither clumsy nor confusing.

They were the kisses of a grown man to his wife. And she had kissed him as a wife would kiss her husband. It was mortifying. It was shameful. It was…intriguing.

Carefully she felt along her hairline, over her face, across her brow, searching for injuries, intent upon finding a lump on her head that would indicate a cracked and fractured skull. It was the only possible explanation.

Darcy paced the inn's narrow corridor, silently cursing his inability to do anything useful. When Elizabeth collapsed, unconscious at his feet, he nearly panicked. The next hour —of stopping his carriage, of finding an inn, of demanding a physician, treatment, anything—while Elizabeth lay unresponsive and pale, was the most dreadful of his life.

Worse, he had no idea what sort of toxic brew Mrs Bennet had administered, and thus could only tell the doctor the symptoms of it. The man administered some sort of purgative, and only half-conscious, Elizabeth began retching again. It was horrible, but the doctor's firm opinion was that once she rid her body of the poison, her current weakness would be resolved by rest and proper diet. While undoubtedly sensible, Darcy's worry and guilt only increased.

He had lost his vaunted control of his temper, of his emotions; he had stooped to mean jealousy, to ridiculous and unkind argument, resentfully blaming Elizabeth for being unable to see through Wickham's machinations. How could she? His own father had been blind to them; the more innocent and good his victim, the less likely they were to see him for the scoundrel he was.

Does she despise me now? He could hardly blame her if she did. His own feelings were ever clearer; seeing her collapse, wondering whether she was at death's door, only emphasised just how much she meant to him.

Life, he knew, was altogether too short for far too many; his father had never seen his fiftieth birthday. His mother had not lived to see forty.

The maid who had been sitting with Elizabeth emerged from her room, interrupting his pacing.

"Your wife be awake, sir," she said. "I be fetching a tray for her now, sir, just as ye wisht."

"Thank you," he replied with a twinge of guilt at his falsehood. He could hardly reveal the truth, however—that he had plucked a young lady away from her mother and groom because she had been poisoned into accepting a fool.

He knew he ought not to enter Elizabeth's room; he was not truly her husband, after all. Yet, until he could see for himself that she was in her right mind, recovering, he would be stretched between the unbearable agonies of doubt and dread.

Just a few words, that I might know she will be well, he thought, and opened the door.

It took his eyes a few moments to adjust to the gloom, but finally he made out the slight figure upon the bed.

"Mr Darcy!" Elizabeth said, her voice sounding both weak and alarmed. Her expressive eyes darted around the room, as if she looked for a means of escape. She was, plainly, anxious—and yet, she faced him bravely.

His heart, which alternated between pumping too hard and stopping entirely, melted. He pulled up a spindly wooden chair to sit beside the bed. In the dim shadows, he saw one slender hand lift slightly from the blankets. Unable to help himself, he took it within his own, and was relieved when she did not pull it away.

"The servant," she said in almost a whisper, "she said that we are—we are married."

"Well, yes," he said, wondering how to explain. "It was necessary to tell the innkeeper, due to what happened."

"What happened?" she repeated, her voice wary. "I cannot remember much of anything. Was there an accident?"

He was determined, this time, that the conversation might not devolve to accusations. "You were given a medication meant for your father, in order to soften your feelings towards matrimony. I believe you were given too much."

"Given *what*? Surely you would not—"

"No, no," he protested immediately. "Not by me. I-I heard of the plot, and only meant to stop your marriage to Mr Collins, your cousin, while you were not in your right mind."

She was quiet for some moments. "I remember him... talking and talking," she said at last. "He would not stop talking. Mama was there, too. Mama."

He said nothing in reply; she had drawn her own conclusions, plainly.

"So...*you* married me instead?"

She sounded bewildered, her voice trembling—the voice of a woman who was holding herself together on sheer will. Darcy knew he had only one chance to get this right.

"To call you wife would be an honour and privilege for any man. I understand you do not know me well. I beg that I might be given a chance to earn your respect." He stopped himself from saying more of his love, his admiration and devotion. She loved another, and he was the only one who knew how futile were her feelings for the despicable Wickham. His earlier jealousy, spoken aloud, had been poorly done, his worst self on display. He did not *wish* to be that man, and prayed she would never remember it.

Her eyes were wide in the dimness. "You are forced, then, by your conscience, into matrimony."

"I do not consider myself forced, but am wretched that you must feel so. I am only resolved to protect your name by any means and to any extent necessary."

"And your own?"

He thought about how to reply. "My name is such that it will weather many storms. Please, allow it to shield you now."

"It is past the point, I suppose, where I have any choice."

The words were bitter—and yet her hand clutched his, giving him hope that she did not find him utterly repulsive.

It was not quite so dire as her words implied, he knew—they might yet escape the situation with everyone's choices intact. If he had thought to give an alias to the doctor and innkeeper, the odds would have been even better that they might remain unrecognised and anonymous. Nevertheless, he was not sorry that in his distress and anxiety at her collapse, he had cast his own reputation and protection over her, and he wished her to prepare herself for the necessity of marriage should it come to that. He opened his mouth to explain it all—as he should probably have done from the beginning—but was interrupted by a knock on the door.

"I has your tray," the servant said, entering at his command.

"Yes, thank you," he said, turning back to Elizabeth. "Please, try and eat something. The doctor recommended plain broth and toast, feeling you would recover your strength quickly if you could eat."

Nourishment and rest, as the doctor had advised, was what was most required at the moment. Fuller explanation could wait. Reluctantly, he let go of her hand, and forced himself to take his leave of her.

Mr Darcy did not return, although she admitted to herself that she waited for him to do so after finishing her bland meal. Her mind alternatively raced and moved sluggishly as she sifted through broken and cracked memories.

There were too many frightening ones.

As best she could remember and piece together, her mother had been behind an attempt to *marry* her to Mr Collins. How very like Mama, neglecting not only to take her daughter's feelings into consideration, but failing to consider that ingesting so much of Papa's tonic might be dangerous!

How could she have done it? Is her understanding so mean, her will so pitiless, that she would throw me away at any cost? She might have ruined my mind, or murdered me outright!

Mr Collins, in her memory, was vacuous, vague, and voluble. It was incredible and yet unsurprising that he could not have understood her to be out of her wits, but then, he truly cared only for himself.

But Mama, Mr Collins, even concern for her ailing Papa possessed only minor bits of her attention. Again and again, she returned to the fantastic idea that somehow Mr Darcy had married her. Somehow, *she* had married Mr Darcy.

Elizabeth had no doubt that the very notion of matrimony was against his wishes and will. Also, she was certain Mr Darcy had not taken advantage of the situation to do it. That entire idea made no sense whatsoever. If he did not precisely hate her, he certainly was no admirer—and with his wealth, excellent birth, and outward beauty, he could obviously have his pick of brides more attractive and affluent.

She had not liked him, it was true—had been well on her way, in fact, to despising him for his mistreatment of her friend, Mr Wickham. But the recollection of this mistreatment, in fact, was what led her to the deepest mystery of all.

How could he disregard the friend of his youth so callously, while showing such extraordinary concern for me? At the ball, he had refused to defend himself from her accusations—conveyed when she ought to have been dancing, not pressing him for explanation—regarding Mr Wickham. *On the other hand, why should he have? What am I to him, that I should deserve to hear any vindication of his motives or actions? I am an insect beneath his shoe.*

An insect he had kissed in a wild, passionate manner, and inexplicably married while she was out of her senses, in order to protect her.

Her head ached. Nothing made sense, no matter how she wrestled with her fractured memories. Finally, she fell into a deep, if troubled sleep.

CHAPTER 7

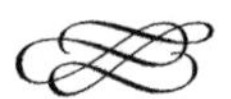

Despite the beauty of the chilly November afternoon, George Wickham was restless. The other officers, even Denny, were jealous of him, leaving him to his own devices more and more often. Chafing at the inaction and lack of opportunities in Meryton and its surrounds, he found few marks available for a man of his talents—and now that Darcy was in the vicinity, he must keep his head lower than ever. The few unsatisfying flirtations he had managed had done nothing to satiate his appetites, and there were far more concerned mamas and papas lurking round every corner than available females willing to risk reputation for a bit of sport.

Speaking of which, one of the noisiest of those mothers was currently marching up the street, looking as militant as any soldier in the regiment. Had Napoleon himself dared pop up before her, she would have obliterated him with one strike of her swinging reticule.

"Mrs Bennet," he called in his most charming voice. "How lovely to see you on a fine November's day. Meryton is quite dull today, as everyone exhausted themselves last evening. Do not tell me that *you* failed to dance until dawn? If only I had been able to attend, I should have made certain you were never lacking a partner."

Her expression lost a degree of chill, as he had known it would.

"If only you *had* been there!" Mrs Bennet cried. "You might have put that awful Mr Darcy in his place! There is no one to stop him now!"

At that moment, a breathless, heavyset young man caught up to her—Mr Collins, Wickham remembered. A vicar now, but the future heir of Longbourn. Envy twisted in his malevolent soul.

"Dear, dear! Stop Darcy from doing what, good madam?" Wickham asked.

She opened her mouth to speak, but Collins beat her to it.

"From stealing my bride," he said sourly. "Mr Darcy has eloped with the faithless, fickle Miss Elizabeth Bennet."

Wickham's brows rose as high as they could go.

Mrs Bennet gave Collins a quelling stare. "We are on our way to my brother Philips," she explained. "He must lend us his carriage. We shall follow the couple and ensure that the nuptials are performed. My Lizzy is entirely blameless in this matter, and if Mr Darcy believes he can make away with my daughter without repercussion, I will give him something else to think about!"

Wickham nearly burst into laughter—as if this foolish pair could possibly exert *any* influence over Darcy! The man could not be bought nor bullied into doing anything he did not wish. *I should know.*

There *must* be more to this supposed 'elopement' than these two were admitting. Darcy would never approve of an elopement of any kind, not for any reason—Wickham also knew *that* all too well.

For that matter, neither could he envision Miss Elizabeth Bennet indulging in any kind of improper behaviour. *If she were the sort, I would certainly have already indulged with her!*

Nevertheless, Darcy's honour often could be used against him, as had been proved in times past. Miss Elizabeth and Darcy were caught up in *something,* and Darcy was unlikely to want her hurt. Oh, they could never force him to a marriage he did not wish—no one could, else he would already be wed to the de Bourgh chit.

No, whatever had happened between Darcy and Miss Elizabeth, Darcy would expect to use his wealth and influence to remove all stain. Wickham did not pretend that Darcy could not succeed. However, the more witnesses there were to this supposed infraction of society's rules, the costlier it would be. If Mrs Bennet and Collins were the only ones who knew of it, Darcy could escape practically unscathed. If, however, someone whom Darcy could *not* trust to keep his mouth shut—at least, not without significant incentive—were to witness him in a potentially scandalous situation, why, Wickham could almost guarantee he would pay. And pay. And pay.

"I will escort you," he offered handsomely. "I know just how to find him in town. I was practically raised with him, you know."

It was dark when Elizabeth wakened, still a trifle disoriented, but feeling much more herself. The same servant, again, was dozing in the chair, and again wakened instantly when she—carefully this time—sat up.

"You're awake!"

"Good evening, Molly," she said. "You have had a very dull day of it, I am afraid."

"It's happy I am to have a dull one, every now and again," the girl said kindly. "And your husband's been paying me well to have it. Is ye hungry?"

Elizabeth thought about this. "You know, I think I am. Perhaps something more substantial than broth? I truly feel much better."

Molly seemed uncertain about whether such a meal would be allowed, but obediently left to ask 'himself'—or so Elizabeth assumed.

Cautiously she stood, noting with distaste that her frock—never one of her favourites—was wrinkled beyond belief. In her stocking feet, she took several experimental steps around the small room, pleased to find that she was now quite steady. Molly returned with a tray—soup again, but a much heartier version. Once the meal was consumed, Elizabeth felt almost her usual self.

Molly carried out the empty dishes, promising to give assurances to 'himself' that she was really quite restored.

With the return of her health, Elizabeth's mind fastened again on the problem at hand, and the many questions begging to be answered. *What kind of character has Mr Darcy? Why did he rescue me from Mama's designs? If he is honourable enough to the point of marrying me in the process of saving me from Mr Collins, why did he treat Mr Wickham so abominably? Why did he* marry *me?*

Besides all that, there were so many important details absent from her splintered memories. Who even had married them? Mr Palmer? Her mind was fuzzy on the order of things, but she remembered being at Longbourn with Mama and Mr Collins and then riding in a carriage. There had been a licence, she somehow recalled, although she could not remember any details about why she knew this. Why could she not remember a ceremony, or even the foggiest notion of a church? There was a memory of a stranger, an older man, offering her a peppermint. Was he a vicar?

At that moment, she spied her half-boots resting beside the hearth.

These were questions only Mr Darcy could answer, and she was no child, afraid of treading the stairs of a respectable establishment in search of him. He might not be in a private parlour, or even the tavern proper. If that were the case, however, someone could fetch him from his room, could they not? She donned her shoes.

A glance in the mirror, unfortunately, told her that her hair was a wild mess, her dark curls having taken on a life of their own—and there was no brush available to tame it. It would be best to wait for Molly, and ask her to obtain an audience with her benefactor. *My husband.* My husband? *It seems impossible.*

She waited. And waited. The girl did not return.

Her impatience with the entire situation grew to unbearable proportions. Finally, she freshened herself as best she could with the bowl and pitcher of water provided, and quickly left the warmth and quiet of the small chamber before she could change her mind.

"Mr Darcy!" cried a snivelling voice. "Where is my bride?"

Darcy sighed. He knew he ought to have waited for a private parlour to empty, but in his relief at hearing of Elizabeth's apparent recovery, he had opted to forego one in favour of immediate fortification. He had been nearly trembling with relief and elation at the news of her improvement. Reluctantly, he turned to face his accuser.

"She never was your bride, idiot," he said—not bothering with politeness.

A second person rounded on him. *Wonderful. A duet of dunderheads. Just what Elizabeth does not need—a public spectacle.*

"What have you done with my daughter?" Mrs Bennet shrieked.

"I do not know what you are talking about."

Her eyes narrowed, and she looked as though she might begin beating him with her reticule. Every person in the inn—including Molly, he abruptly noticed, who was *supposed* to be waiting on Elizabeth—turned to stare at them.

"Tell me now or I shall search every room in the place!" she screeched.

He would not allow it—and nor, he suspected, would the innkeeper, whose bushy brows were already drawn together in a frown. This was a respectable inn, and the attention they were drawing was anything but.

"Listen to me," he growled in the low tones of one accustomed to deference, his eyes narrowed in wrathful command. "If either of you have a brain in your head, you will turn round immediately, and walk out that door. There is *no one* here. Everyone is safe. Everything you desire shall be returned to you with no harm done, but only if you *quietly* leave. Do it. *Now!*"

The last word was uttered with such vehemence that the two before him quailed, slumping accordingly into a compliant obedience. In fact, everyone in the entire room seemed to find something or someone else to look at.

That is right. Nothing to see here. As long as they departed without a fuss, there was unlikely to be any scandal. He could maintain Elizabeth's choices for her, as he was honour bound to do, and which he knew she would prefer. His own preferences mattered little in comparison.

But into that sudden quiet, a soft voice emerged. "Mr Darcy, I would speak with you, please." He swivelled to meet it. Elizabeth—lovelier than he had ever before seen, pink-cheeked, her long hair tumbling and curling over her slim shoulders and a crumpled dress, looking for all the world as if she had just emerged from his bed after a long day of play—stood at the inn's stairwell.

"Mama? Mr Collins?" she questioned, her confusion obvious when they, too, turned to look at her.

And then the awful voice, the voice he hated most in all the world, the voice of one he had wished beyond reason that he would never have to hear again, called out loudly, derision in every word.

"Well, well, well, Darcy. How fortunate that I spotted your carriage. Methinks the cat has been caught cavorting with the canary, with a few sweet feathers still sticking to his lips."

Elizabeth was not stupid. She heard and understood Mr Wickham's insinuation; she supposed he might be excused for some misinterpretation of the circumstances, but she did not appreciate his blatantly coarse—and loudly stated—assumptions.

Darcy shot to his feet, glaring, anger pouring from him; he was a good half a head taller than Mr Wickham, who reddened, but did not move away. Mrs Bennet glanced at the two men warily, as if she had just grasped that the situation might be a bit beyond her touch. Mr Collins took an actual step backwards.

"Shut. Your. Mouth," Darcy ordered, his voice low and wrathful.

"Oh, happily," Mr Wickham said smoothly, never even glancing at Elizabeth. "For a price."

Elizabeth gaped. Was this man—whom she had believed a friend, at least, if not a suitor—threatening *extortion*? What if she had been abducted? What if she had *needed* rescue? Apparently, all she could expect from this… this villain, was more trouble.

Darcy did not appear surprised at Mr Wickham's coercion.

"You may toss your lies and allegations at me all day long. I could not care less for the accusations of a worm. One note of caution however: say one more word which implicates or alludes to *anyone else* of *anything* except the highest standards of comportment, and you shall be very sorry indeed."

Darcy had not raised his voice—although with the patrons all so silent, he could be easily heard. Neverthe-less, and despite the softness of his tone, Mr Collins took another step back. Mr Wickham, however, managed a laugh—although she was certain she heard the tension in it and saw the shifting of his feet, as if he were tempted to bolt.

"Who am I to accuse you, my good man? I see nothing

wrong with a bit of bed sport with a willing female—and all females are willing at heart, are they not? If you have finally shaken a few feathers from her stingy little tail, 'tis all well and good. I require only a few pounds to forget what I witnessed here."

Darcy moved so quickly, Mr Wickham never saw the punch coming. One moment, the vile man was standing, taunting—the next he was on the floor, blood dripping from his nose, his face a wreck of damaged cartilage. He scrambled to his knees, attempting to rise, spewing curses —but Elizabeth had had enough.

"You contemptible vermin!" she hissed, going at once to Darcy's side. "This is my *husband* whom you accuse. You are unworthy to be standing in the same room with him! It is fortunate indeed that he began with a warning knock—a little tap, really, and only a small portion of the anger and disgust he rightly feels for you."

Mr Wickham sat back down on the floor, looking at her and then at Darcy in astonished disbelief. She heartily wished she had the strength to punch him herself.

"B-but...you cannot be married to *her*!" Mr Collins cried. "You are betrothed to Miss Anne de Bourgh!"

Darcy gave Mr Collins a look such as Elizabeth never hoped to receive, taking a threatening step towards him. He scurried from the room.

Darcy turned to her then, his expression immediately gentling. She held out her hand and he took it, tucking it in the crook of his arm, his dark eyes fathomless.

She glanced at her mother, who appeared strangely

satisfied. "How could you, Mama? How *could* you? You ought to be ashamed of yourself, and I hope you are—but regardless of whether you feel any guilt or regret, I will never agree to receive you after the trouble you have caused my husband. You may tell my papa..." Here, her breath hitched.

Darcy would be well within his rights to cut her off from all her family, and certainly to distrust them—they had forced his unwilling hand. Perhaps in time, she could convince him of the goodness of the Gardiners; she hoped he was not unreasonable. But she would not blame him if it required some years—indeed, she was very fortunate he did not hate *her* along with them. "Tell Papa to quit taking that awful tonic, and he will likely be well in no time at all. And Jane..."

She could not manage a message for Jane. She would burst into tears and might never stop crying if she thought too much of her sister. "I will write to her," she said. She looked up at...at her husband. "Shall we?" she asked.

He nodded soberly.

Together, arm in arm, they walked from the room.

CHAPTER 8

Elizabeth maintained her dignified countenance until the heavy inn door shut firmly behind them and they had walked several steps into the darkness beyond it. Suddenly she stopped, forcing Darcy to pause with her, and looked up at him.

"I have no idea where I am going," she said.

"I was following your lead."

She burst into laughter. "That is not at all wise, sir, when I have been out of my head for most of the day. I suppose your belongings are still at the inn?"

"A few bits and bobs only. Oh, and my man is there, awaiting my return. I suppose he might begin to wonder, if I did not."

She shook her head ruefully. "Let us turn back, then."

"I would never dream of spoiling such a perfect exit as you provided us. I will send someone to fetch him, and my coachman as well."

"It is long past dark, and unfair to drag them out," she worried aloud.

"Probably the innkeeper would insist upon our departure regardless—engaging in fisticuffs in his taproom is frowned upon, I am certain. My men will understand, once they know Wickham is in the vicinity. Besides we are a mere couple of hours, give or take, from town, and doubtless they would prefer to have their own beds."

Which they could have had long ago, had they not had to deal with me and my illness, she thought. The fact that Darcy's entire contingent would want to remove him from Mr Wickham's vicinity was no longer surprising.

Matching words to action, he gained the attention of a stableman, who promptly ran to do his bidding. People had a way of doing that, she noticed. In fact, it seemed like no time at all before once again, they were ensconced in his carriage, rumbling along the pavement. Moonlight flooded the vehicle, lighting the interior and yet Darcy remained cloaked in gloom.

Elizabeth had more questions than answers, but for some reason was reluctant to break the silence between them. He sat across from her, a large, silent, dark silhouette; with almost surprising boldness she heard herself burst out with the last words she had ever thought to utter.

"I wish you were not so far away from me." Realising how brazen she had sounded, she tried to explain. "It is difficult to speak to your shadow."

Instantly he moved into the space beside her, so

quickly it was startling—almost as if he had very much wanted to sit next to her.

Well, she thought, *since we are married, there is no reason why we should not begin to be comfortable with each other.* And so she leant against him, and was gratified when he moved his arm around her and covered her hand with his much larger one. It was an unfamiliar feeling, to be resting in the arms of a man.

It was also sweet, satisfying some need she had never known she possessed.

"I am sure you require explanations," he said, but then did not offer any.

"Yes," she agreed.

More silence.

"Who is Anne de Bourgh?" she asked at last. It was the least of the questions brimming in her thoughts—but *if* he possessed an affianced bride, one that probably ought to be addressed quickly.

He made a small noise of displeasure. "She is my cousin. I can assure you, we never *were* betrothed, although my aunt likes to pretend it is so, no matter how often I remind her otherwise."

"That must be annoying," she replied. "I—"

"I am so sorry," he interrupted, and his words spilled out in a sudden rush. "I am sorry for Wickham's insinuations, and for losing command of myself so completely that you were forced to witness violence. Further, if there is any way you could forget our argument, the things I said to you concerning him earlier today, I would be grateful beyond reason. I meant *none* of it."

"Your wish has already been granted," Elizabeth said, after a moment's bewilderment. "I have no recollection of any argument. My memories are random and erratic, having more to do with events that perhaps occurred earlier in the day? We argued about...Mr Wickham?"

He sighed. "I am unsure you were arguing at all. It was I who...behaved poorly at the mention of his name."

She thought about this, trying so hard to remember, it almost hurt. There was hardly anything, beyond the vague, nonsensical recollections of her mother, of Mr Collins, of the peppermints, and kissing Darcy. *Some parts of the past, I think, probably ought to stay happily buried; no doubt he, too, has had cause this day to be upset*. "I truly have no recollection of this quarrel. Mr Wickham behaved despicably this evening, however, and I shall henceforth call him no friend of mine. I suppose it is possible that he might spread rumours about me within his regiment, but my family's name is a good one. Hopefully he would not be believed."

"As to that," said Darcy, "I doubt he will return to Meryton. He does not usually behave so callously before witnesses, but his greed got the better of him, imagining, as he did, that he had caught me in a compromising situation."

"You were rescuing me! He is a churl!"

"In the end, it was your quick thinking that achieved the rescue."

Elizabeth could not see how quick thinking had

entered into it, but before she could ask, he continued speaking. "I should perhaps better account for the, er, depth of my hostility. Wickham was a great favourite with my father, but my friendship with him was finished while still a schoolboy."

"I have heard his claim that your father left him a legacy, a valuable living—but you would not give it to him. I suppose he lied."

"Only if he neglected to mention that he was paid three thousand pounds to sign away any rights to it."

She sat up straight, looking at him. "Truly? Why, it is positively criminal to make such claims on you now, then!"

But he only sighed again. "That, along with another thousand my father left him, satisfied the monetary requirements of the will. But he wanted the obligations and commitment of family...to the point of attempting an elopement with my fifteen-year-old sister. I have no doubt of your secrecy on this matter—I only hope you might more fully understand how the very mention of him creates misery for me. I will admit that I have wished to throw that punch for several months now, and was finally given an excuse."

His young sister? Elizabeth could only gape, shaking her head in disbelief. "No," she whispered. "He is a monster."

He hesitated, piercing her with the intensity of his gaze even in the dim carriage, and then added, "Especially when it is you who shows interest in him. There is no excuse for my jealousy—it was never within your power to understand how great a scoundrel he is, and I certainly enlightened no one."

We argued over Wickham because Darcy was jealous?

"That seems incredible. Before today, you did not even like me."

He huffed a soft breath of what might have been laughter, and before she could even realise what had happened, his mouth was on hers, his big hands alternately framing her face or his fingertips threading through her hair, stroking her scalp.

At first Elizabeth was shocked, holding still as a trapped bird, her heart beating wildly. Yet, the astonishment could not remain, not with the taste of him, the heat of his mouth, igniting a fervour in her blood. Before she knew she would even *want* to touch him, her own hands were seeking, tracing the breadth of his shoulders, searching, even slipping beneath his coat to find more of his precious warmth and closeness. It was the kiss from her memories except more, even, as if the fire of his passion had kindled ever more hotly in the interim, striking sparks everywhere they touched.

"In case you were unsure," he said, spreading kisses up her jaw to a delicious place below her ear, "I have been dying for this—to hold you, to kiss you, to make you mine."

"I cannot think," she murmured. "I cannot tell whether I am still dizzy or if I have forgotten how to breathe."

At her words, he halted mid-kiss, tilting his head back

to look at her. After a moment, he let a breath out, resting his forehead against hers.

"I am a beast," he said. "You have been ill."

"You are my husband," she said softly. "You need not stop. Although we do have a problem—I am not of age. I suppose my father will not challenge it, however, and would give his permission after the fact."

But at this he reared back. "What did you say?"

Elizabeth was confused by his obvious astonishment. "I am only twenty. It is yet a good four months until my birth—"

"We are not married!"

"You said we were!"

He gaped. "I am sure I never did."

"I could hardly have made up such a thing! You said it!" Realising that she was still seated on his lap, she hurriedly moved off onto the upholstered bench.

Elizabeth was mortified. *Had* she imagined it? Were his words a mere product of her imagination and illness? But no, she was certain!

"You spoke of the honour and privilege of marrying me, when I regained consciousness at the inn. It was almost the first thing you said to me. I am sure you did!" She grimaced. "I think."

His brow smoothed, a hint of white teeth showing her a slight smile. "And so it would be both honour and privilege. You misunderstood me, my dear. I said that I told the innkeeper we were married, justifying our travel alone together. I only meant to explain to you that a marriage might become necessary, if circumstances did not permit our remaining anonymous. Many know me. These things have a way of getting out—as you know, now, for yourself."

"You did not argue the marriage when I announced it to my mother and Wickham!"

He gathered up her hands in his, holding on when she would have pulled away. "Of course I did not. You were brilliant. I will get a licence and we will quickly turn the lie into truth."

She stared at him. "What you mean is that from the moment you heard of Mama's plotting, you were doomed, your choices surrendered. What you mean is that I have forced you into a marriage, without your consent."

"Rather, I think it was the push I needed, to take the step I wanted. I stupidly allowed the inferiority of your connexions and that total want of propriety so frequently displayed by your mother and your three younger sisters to stand in the way of my feelings."

Elizabeth saw it then, all too clearly. He had been attracted to her, perhaps deeply attracted. But mere desire would *never* have been enough for him. He had expected to...to do better.

"In other words, had you not been forced by your conscience to rescue me, you would never have asked me to marry you. There are trunks atop this carriage. You were already packed when you received word of this plot by Mama and Mr Collins. You would have departed Netherfield and never looked back."

Even in the near-darkness, she could tell his gaze slid away from hers; her heart dropped to her half-boots.

"What does that signify? I was wrong. My eyes have been opened."

"Your desires have been tempted. It is not a good enough reason."

"A few minutes ago, it was," Darcy said, jaw clenching. "You were prepared to accept the marriage when you did not recall it."

She tugged her hands away from his. "I was prepared to make the best of an unfortunate situation. I trusted that if you said we must be married, we must already be."

"And so we must. You have announced the marriage to your mother—not known for her discretion—and who else heard, one can only guess. Collins, for one, has seen you in a disreputable circumstance. Will he be quiet? Not to mention Wickham."

"My father can enforce my mother's silence. Mr Collins is a fool—I cannot believe anyone would care for a word he utters. Mr Wickham believes us to be wed, and you have already said he is unlikely to return to Meryton to learn differently. If you take me to my uncle Gardiner in Cheapside, I can stay with my 'inferior connexions' until it all blows over and some new scandal comes along for small minds to fuss about. It might take some time, but if nothing comes of this incident, it will all be forgotten eventually."

"You and Miss Bennet must always be excluded from

any like criticism of inferiority," he said. "I did not mean to insult you."

"Of course you did not. To you, it is simply truth—you are of one rank, and I am of another, a much lower one. My portion is abysmal, my nearest relations are embarrassing. Imagining Mama as your mother-in-law is unbearably preposterous. Why would you do anything else *except* depart and call it a lucky escape?"

He appeared to be struggling to find words to refute hers. And then he said ones she had not expected. "Because I love you."

Almost, she threw herself back into his arms. It was the first time anyone had ever made such a declaration to her, and she was mightily tempted to hold onto it, to treasure it...to *believe* it. But she had an education in this particular circumstance that he likely did not. Briefly she touched the roughness of his cheek, her heart breaking, her conscience forcing her to be truthful, to *not* do the easy thing.

"My father fell in love with my mother many years ago, and nothing would do but that he should quickly marry her. Relating it now, it always becomes a cautionary tale to his daughters. They have been very unhappy together, I think. What you and I feel for each other is desire, an apparently fleeting emotion that cannot survive the first year of wedlock."

"Thank you for explaining my feelings to me so fully," he said, frustration in his voice. "Has it occurred to you that you might be wrong? That your father will be unable to prevent rumour and scandal, affecting not only you but your sisters as well? That not everyone will think Collins's tales ridiculous? That you might be exposing us both to the world for disgrace and dishonour?"

It was hard to hear the anger and hurt in his tone. It was difficult to consider that her choices now might poorly reflect upon her sisters. She did not know whether she loved him; her feelings had only recently undergone a rapid transformation. But she knew that, once she had accepted as fact a belief that they were married, she had felt neither panic over the future nor distress in the present. Instead, it had been as though she had been handed a gift; upon opening it, she had glimpsed something of inexpressible value, a dream she had never dared to dream.

Now she was tossing the gift back at him, as if it were worthless.

"I do this for you," she made herself say. "Your honour demands immediate action—you are literally *unable* to do aught but try to protect me. I also do this for me—lest with any and every future disagreement, I wonder how many regrets you harbour over this day."

His jaw firmed at her words as the silence grew fraught between them. Abruptly, however, he sighed. In that sigh, she heard acceptance.

He sees the sense in it now, she thought, even as regret filled her. Had she wanted him to argue? Refuse to take 'no' for an answer?

Yes, her fickle heart answered for her. Yet, her sensible brain realised his cooperation was for the best.

For what seemed an endless time, they sat in a silence grown miserable, at least to her—side by side, but as if a brick wall had arisen between them. The well-sprung carriage swayed with the undulations of a rough patch of road beneath the wheels.

"Can you give me your uncle's direction? I will relay it to Frost at our next stop."

It was nothing less than what she had asked for—to be taken elsewhere, away from him. But regret was an ache in her heart and a lump in the pit of her throat. Quietly, she gave him the information. He only nodded in response, and silence fell again.

The night was cold. She had not noticed it before, but now that she had no distractions it was positively frigid. She wrapped her arms around herself, wretched, and tried not to think, not to remember, not to hurt.

But his words would not leave her mind.

"To call you wife would be an honour and privilege for any man. I understand you do not know me well. I beg that I might be given a chance to earn your respect."

"I have been dying for this—to hold you, to kiss you, to make you mine."

"Because I love you."

She was trying so hard to do what was right, what was best—only to have his words haunting and taunting the honour she attempted. In situations such as these, a good memory was unpardonable! Why was it so difficult to leave him, when she had known him so little? Yesterday, she had thought them practically enemies! Beyond that, she was fatigued, heartsick, and freezing. The first tear fell, and then another. She did her best to weep silently, desperately not wanting him to know, but even a small sniffle sounded loud in the quiet between them. Perhaps, however, he would politely pretend not to notice, thereby leaving her dignity intact.

"Elizabeth," he said, his voice low. "Come here." He turned towards her, breaching the invisible distance, pulling her into his arms.

Instead of refusing as she ought, she went easily, burrowing into his warmth willingly, allowing him to cradle her unresistingly as he wrapped the edges of his greatcoat around her and held her close.

"You are so cold," he said, by way of excuse for both of them. It was an insufficient one; he might have offered to give her the coat instead.

But it was the last time she would ever feel his arms around her, safe and soothing. One final memory to cherish, as the sound of horse hooves and the grind of carriage wheels against the gravel, his strong heartbeat beneath her head, created an odd sort of lullaby. Her tears dried almost instantly on her cheeks within the peace of it, and —though she tried to fight it, to stay awake, to relish every remaining moment—between one breath and the next, she slept.

CHAPTER 9

Darcy held Elizabeth in his arms for the rest of the journey. She stirred a bit when Frost stopped just beyond the outskirts of London, but he was able to give directions to Gracechurch Street without waking her. She was exhausted, the poor girl; he admitted, if only to himself, that he was glad of it. Had she possessed her full strength, she would never have allowed him to continue the embrace—even though it was only Frost, his trusted coachman, who saw it.

In the meantime, he memorised every inch of her face in the unsatisfactory flashes of carriage lantern lights through the window—high cheekbones, perfectly shaped lips he longed to kiss again, thick lashes resting against the pale, perfect beauty of her skin.

He wanted her, oh yes, that. Holding her like this was exquisite torture. Yet, it was not all desire, as she feared.

How stupid I was, to remind her of the flaws of her mother and sisters when she already was feeling such mortification! She truly was the victim of her mother's machinations, had already made clear that she did not expect him to receive Mrs Bennet—and while her sisters had shown themselves to be undisciplined, that, too, was a failing of their parents. Elizabeth's behaviour was always faultless, as was her elder sister's.

It was not as though his own family was perfect. His uncle, though an earl, constantly overspent his means, while his aunt, the widow of a wealthy baronet, preferred to talk instead of listen, meddling in the lives of everyone around her without doing anything to improve them. He was powerless to change either of them—indeed, it had never before occurred to him that he ought to try. Why had he even mentioned his distaste for her family members? Had he expected her to rejoice in his critical opinions? No, he had only succeeded in making her feel more deeply their differences, emphasising a fearful approach to the future.

Her father had chosen poorly, a once pretty girl of mean understanding, little information, and uncertain temper. Nevertheless, her eldest daughters were lovely women of charm and steady disposition. To that, Elizabeth added poise, a clever wit, a happy nature, a keen intelligence, and exceptional fortitude. He could not think of another who could have withstood the day she had just endured with such grace and courage.

She had wakened that morning with a poor opinion of him, thanks to Wickham—and thanks to his own refusal to counter any of Wickham's deceits, to give her or anyone else a reason to think better of him. After being *poisoned* by her mother and believing herself married to him, she had nevertheless proceeded to 'make the best of a bad situation'—by joining him in a passion he had never dreamt. Deep down, Elizabeth trusted him—without it, she never could have responded as she had. Many women would be eager to wed him simply due to his wealth and standing; she thought only of whether they could truly be happy together.

She did not wish to repeat her parents' mistakes, of course—but they *could* avoid them. His thoughtless pride had caused their current rift; he only needed to be the gentleman he had been raised to be, to continually show her, by every civility within his power, her importance to him and his respect for her and for those she loved.

Would she give him the opportunity to prove his worth? Would this be the last time he would ever hold her? He did his best to stay fixed in the present, to cherish these moments of closeness—but with every passing minute, he grew more and more aware that he was about to deliver her to unknown relations who may or may not be amenable to his continued interest in her life. He could not know whether they would allow her to stay in London, or if she might be whisked away elsewhere. His future—once so staid, so predictable—had become a great unknown.

Elizabeth did not rouse until the carriage stopped before a well-lit, surprisingly grand home in Gracechurch

Street. Plainly a bit disoriented, she sat up, looking sleepily at him. "We are here already?"

Maintaining an equanimity he did not feel, Darcy brushed her soft cheek with one thumb. "You did not wake when we stopped on the outskirts of town. You are exhausted, and I wanted you to remain asleep if you could."

The carriage door opened then, and he hurried to hand her out himself. Before she could think of a protest, he took her arm so that he might be allowed to accompany her to her uncle's door. A neat servant answered it, and, recognising Elizabeth, greeted her warmly before hurrying to fetch her mistress.

"Lizzy!" her aunt cried. "This is a pleasant surprise!" She stopped short at the sight of him.

"Aunt Gardiner, this is Mr Darcy—a very good friend of Mr Bingley, whom I think I have mentioned in my letters. He has done me a great service today, one which I can hardly repay." She bit her lip, obviously uncertain of what next to say.

He bowed. "It is a pleasure to meet any relation of Miss Elizabeth's. I am certain she will wish to give you lengthier explanations of why we have appeared, unannounced, upon your doorstep. I wonder if her uncle, Mr Gardiner, is at home, that I might have a private word with him? I promise not to take up much of his time."

He was a stranger to these people, and it was an irregular request to be sure, but it was obvious that their presence here was anything except 'regular'. Elizabeth gave him a measuring look, which he did his best to return with a reassuring smile. Whether he was successful or not, he could not say.

One thing was certain—Elizabeth obviously had no reason to be ashamed of either Mr or Mrs Gardiner. Their home was lovely, their decorum flawless, their manners impeccable. Gardiner's study was as elegant as Darcy's own at his Mayfair home; the man himself was immaculately dressed in perfectly tailored clothing. It was with a niggling sense of shame that he recalled his expressions of near contempt to the Bingley sisters. Though many gentlemen refused to have anything to do with trade, he had made several wise investments in promising businesses—and in his inexperience, a few unwise ones as well; he supposed a man like Mr Gardiner seldom made the same errors. *My low assumptions of the Gardiners' respectability were completely mistaken.*

"Thank you for bringing my niece to me, Mr Darcy," Gardiner said politely, once they were both seated. But Darcy heard a note of steely discontent within his mannerly address. This was not a man who would be impressed by the Darcy name or be put off by vague explanation, no matter who gave it. "I admit to a good deal of surprise at finding my favourite niece upon my stoop—and accompanied only by a man with whom I am unfamiliar."

"You may well be—although probably not quite so surprised as I am," Darcy replied ruefully. It was remarkably difficult to know how to tell the tale. "It began this morning, when my man informed me of a plot against

Miss Elizabeth—although I suppose, truthfully, the story starts at a Meryton assembly some weeks ago."

"Your mother did *what?*" Mrs Gardiner had taken Elizabeth aside in her private sitting room, where they would not be disturbed; a tray of tea, biscuits, and breads sat between them. "Lizzy, I can hardly credit it!"

Elizabeth took a bite of a biscuit, staring at it contemplatively. "Believe me when I say that I am now certain she will go to any length to achieve a marriage for one of her daughters. You do not want to know how many times I cast up my accounts between Longbourn and here. She gave me far too large a dose of Papa's tonic, I am certain."

Her aunt looked aghast. "Because she wanted you to agree to a wedding with that cousin you wrote me of? It seems too fantastic for words."

"I agree! Especially because I was, in essence, drunk as a sailor. Only Mr Collins would be so stupid as to have failed to realise it. In my memories, the entire world was spinning madly. I am sure I seemed absolutely nonsensical."

"I cannot believe any parson would conduct such a ceremony."

"I wish I could not believe it, but he apparently had a licence and old Mr Palmer… Let us just say that I have had a very near escape, thanks to Mr Darcy's quick actions."

"Mr Darcy," Mrs Gardiner repeated thoughtfully. "I

grew up in Lambton, which was near a grand estate, Pemberley, owned by a Mr George Darcy. I wonder if he is the son?"

"I have heard Pemberley praised by Miss Bingley. It must be the same family."

"If so, Lizzy, he is a great man, indeed. Pemberley is beyond anything."

Mrs Gardiner was no stranger to the finer things in life; for her to compliment Pemberley in such words was significant. For a moment, Elizabeth could not suppress a streak of longing to see it; in the next minute, the memory of her mother's unconscionable behaviour became that much more embarrassing, the differences between herself and Darcy growing that much more vast. "I suppose that explains his general contempt for our little society," she said, trying to make sense of it. "He has not been amiable —indeed, even yesterday I would have said he hated us all." At her aunt's expression, she suddenly felt the need to defend him. "However, he has recently dealt with troubles in his family that would dampen anyone's spirits. Indeed, he has had much weight upon his shoulders."

Mrs Gardiner gave her a shrewd look. "I must say, you do not seem nearly as distressed about the experience as I would expect you to be—nor so angry with your mother as she probably deserves."

Elizabeth sighed. "Oh, I am furious with her, never doubt it—furious and mortified. But other matters also occupy my thoughts. You see, Mama's guile is only the beginning of my tale."

Elizabeth told her aunt the whole of it—almost. She did not share anything of kisses, nor of hours spent in his arms. But she told her of falling ill and being taken to an inn, and believing, in her confusion and stupor, that she and Mr Darcy were married, of the surprising feelings of acceptance, and the subsequent confrontation at the inn with Mr Wickham, her mother, and Mr Collins. She told her of learning otherwise—and how Mr Darcy had gallantly offered for her.

"I believe that he might even now be suggesting to my uncle that we be married immediately," Elizabeth finished. "He strongly feels there is a chance that my reputation is at grave risk, due to our stop at the inn, and the confrontation that took place there."

Her aunt shook her head in astonishment. "This is...an incredible day you have had, Lizzy," she said, with massive understatement. "Nevertheless, it is just one day. I am certain your uncle will advise that we all take an interval of recovery and see how the world responds to your, um, adventure. Such a marriage may not be at all necessary, especially if you remain with us for a nice, long visit, allowing the situation to cool. However, should the worst happen, at least he is respectable—beyond respectable, even."

"I will not marry him, Auntie," Elizabeth insisted. "He is being heroic, and saddling himself with a bride he could not possibly want, and all because Mama, once again, has behaved appallingly, and this time, dragged me into her horrid scheming."

Mrs Gardiner took her time responding. "I agree that it would be difficult to accept a marriage proposal out of gratitude, and given for reasons beyond, almost, imagination. However, Lizzy, allow me to caution you—do not allow your pride to make such an important decision on your behalf. If you believe him to be a good man you could like and respect, why not allow those feelings to grow into a foundation for happiness?"

That is the problem, Elizabeth would admit only to herself. *I could love him so easily—but how could* he *love a bride foisted upon him by deception?* But she did not say so aloud, lest her aunt accuse her again of having too much pride. Perhaps she did—but such an unequal connexion must surely lead to resentment instead of happiness!

"It is late," her aunt suddenly said briskly. "You must be weary beyond belief. I have had your usual room prepared for you. You are not to think of anything else except rest and recovery. I ought to have put you to bed immediately and left these explanations for morning."

In no time at all, Elizabeth was donning a borrowed gown and tucked into a comfortable bed. Sleep, however, was a long time in coming.

CHAPTER 10

Darcy wakened the next morning with a good deal of hopefulness. Elizabeth's relations were the exact sort of people he most respected—polished and mannerly. Gardiner, while not being at all brash, had assured him that he would not allow Elizabeth's reputation to suffer any damage. He seemed to appreciate Darcy's intention to see everything put right, and while not agreeing to any talk about settlements, he would likely be an ally in promoting marriage, should the scandal bloom and Elizabeth continue to resist.

Elizabeth was not resisting out of any dearth of feeling, Darcy judged—but because he had not done anything before this point to court her. She must think his feelings for her were new and motivated only by his rescue and a few kisses. If a scandal resulted, she would continue to believe he offered *only* because of it.

The best course of action—at least, according to

Gardiner—was to leave her at Gracechurch Street and resist encouraging that possible scandal. If one did not arise, she could hardly suppose Darcy to be forced by it, could she? Unfortunately, this meant he must stay away from them all until such time as the situation could be presumed to be resolved.

Nonetheless, he had made clear to Gardiner his intentions—that he wished for Elizabeth to become his wife. He hoped the man believed him to be sincere, and that his motivations had nothing to do with dishonour or possible rumours. He was not quite sure that her uncle was convinced, but time would prove his friend in this matter.

Two weeks, he had agreed to keep his distance—unless Gardiner discovered that rumours had begun. Two long, endless weeks. He would not be idle, however. There was a settlement to prepare—he meant to see that his future wife was kept and cared for as well as if she had been the heiress he had expected. He would bring Georgiana to town from Matlock, where she currently resided with her governess, Mrs Annesley, and prepare her for the possibility of a new sister. Come to think of it, the mistress' suite of rooms in both town and at Pemberley were much in need of refurbishing. Elizabeth would probably prefer to do them herself, but at least in his Mayfair home, he could see the faded wallpapers removed and have the walls painted. Something lighter, he thought. Making and carrying out these plans would pass the next weeks, albeit slowly; he dared not think too much about how he would possibly fill the rest of his life, should she continue to refuse him.

First thing the next morning, Elizabeth wrote a lengthy letter to her father—at her uncle's request—describing what had occurred in every particular.

"I do not know whether he will read it," Elizabeth said. "He mostly sleeps."

"Your description of this tonic he has been ingesting convinces me that he must cease taking it," Mr Gardiner replied. "I will deliver the letter to Longbourn myself. I have a few choice words for my sister—and Mr Collins, if he is still there. I will remain at Longbourn until I am certain your father is in his right mind, and tell him exactly how I feel about the management of his household. It is high time he set it to rights."

"You might never return, if you intend to wait for that happy day," Elizabeth replied, with a little bitterness.

Mr Gardiner smiled. "I shall return within a few days, I think. If this whole mess does not bring Bennet to his senses, nothing will. He will see the disaster this could have been, had your mother been successful in her plotting. It does not bear considering."

As the days passed, Elizabeth could not help wondering if Mr Darcy would call, or send a note to her uncle, or make some...gesture. She told herself she was being foolish to expect it. He had not wanted a bride before accidentally abducting one. If he could release her without incident, he would surely do so. And yet, with every caller, her heart leapt before she could prevent it, and disappointment welled before she could beat it back.

Late in the afternoon of the fifth day of his absence, Mr Gardiner returned. He looked…tired.

"Uncle? Are you well?"

He kissed his wife's cheek and withdrew a letter from his inner coat pocket, handing it to Elizabeth. "I am absolutely well, and even better now that I have returned to my favourite place in the world. I must look in on my warehouses, but I shall pop up to the nursery before I do so and greet the children."

"And give them the treats your pockets are doubtless full of? Edward, you will spoil their dinners." But there was no heat in her words as Mrs Gardiner smiled fondly at her husband. He winked at her and made his way upstairs. Patting Elizabeth on the shoulder, Mrs Gardiner tactfully left her alone with her letter and followed him.

Such a great sympathy existed between her aunt and uncle! It was just what she had always wanted for herself —but was such a dream even possible?

She looked down at the letter she held; her father's writing was even, not at all shaky nor betraying any weakness, and containing two sheets of letter paper, written quite through, in a very close hand. The envelope itself was likewise full. Carefully, she unsealed it, and began to read.

My Dearest Daughter,

Your recent letter has succeeded in astonishing me exceedingly. Of course, your uncle did not give it to me until yesterday, after directing, upon his arrival, that I should take no more of the heart tonic prescribed by Mr Jones. I have only the vaguest memories of the last two weeks; therefore, I must accept as fact what your mother says—that I gave my signed permission to Mr Collins to procure a licence for a marriage between you and him. I pray you know I was not in my right mind, or it never would have been granted.

Your uncle assures me that you have married neither Mr Collins nor Mr Darcy; nor are you upon the brink of matrimony to any other. Thankfully, he arrived before your mother or her sister Philips could announce a marriage of any sort to the neighbourhood. Mr Collins did not return with her from wherever it was that you met her on the road to London. I shall write to him as soon as I finish this letter to you, and command him to say nothing of any of it. He is unquestionably the weakest link in this chain—now that Mr Wickham has, rumour reports, deserted his regiment—but I cannot think that a vicar in Kent can have so many connexions that he would be able to ruin your good name with such an absurd tale as he possesses. Who, that knows either, would believe that you would elope with Mr Darcy, or that Mr Darcy would elope with you? Had it been any other man, it might have meant great danger; but Mr Darcy's perfect indifference to you—and your pointed dislike of him—shall protect you both. It is to be hoped that Collins's own participation in the affair shall remain likewise unacknowledged.

You may of course write to all your friends here, and announce that your uncle visited and took you back to town with him upon his return. I sent your trunk with him so that you can stay until the new year. Within that period, I expect all potential or possible drama to be cast aside in favour of my other news: Mr Bingley has returned to Netherfield.

I, naturally, had no idea that he had ever departed Netherfield. Your eldest sister received a letter from Miss Bingley the afternoon following your own exodus from Longbourn—announcing that all Bingleys, Darcys, and attendant parties, would be leaving for town and would not be returning—an event which, apparently, cast everyone into a state of despair. But this proved to be untrue, at least insofar as her brother is concerned. Bingley has called twice already, and seems well on his way to an understanding with your sister. Or so I am informed by Mrs Bennet; Jane only smiles and blushes, and has hardly had a useful word to utter since he reappeared upon my doorstep.

Lizzy, your uncle has made sure I understand how mortified you have been made to feel, and how easily either your good name or your future might have been ruined. Even now, to imagine you held hostage as the wife of Mr Darcy, who never looks at any woman except to see a blemish, and who probably never regarded you in his life—until he was forced by some gentlemanly code to come to your rescue—causes me such trembling and fluttering as even your mother has never experienced. Your uncle Gardiner blames me for all of it.

He accuses that I have left the futures of all my daughters solely in your mother's hands, a task which is quite beyond her abilities. Try as I might—and believe me, I have tried—I cannot fault his reasoning. My own health has been mediocre, it is true. Still, whilst I have living breath, I cannot ignore my obligations any longer.

However, neither can I cope with having five daughters out at once; it is too much, and I will not live to see my next birthday should I attempt it. Therefore, only Jane and you are to be given the privilege of appearing in society. This shall remain the rule until the eighteenth birthdays of my younger daughters, when they might be allowed more freedom—and then, only if they demonstrate any small scrap whatsoever of maturity. At present levels of good and common sense, it seems they shall all remain at home for the next decade.

As you can expect, there has been much weeping, wailing, and gnashing of teeth, especially from the two youngest. However, I have threatened to die—and leave them all to present their complaints instead to Mr Collins—if they wail and gnash too loudly. Your mother worries that I might, since quitting Jones's tonic, and thus far has done her best to restrain them. I will not tell her that I am feeling, despite the lack of medicinal dosage, in exceptionally good and cheerful spirits. Your mother, whatever her other failings, has proved an excellent nurse. I trust your discretion with this information, and that you will not undo all her good work by taking part in kidnap, poison, or any other indiscretion for the foreseeable future.

With a quieter social life and fewer dressmakers' bills, who knows but that I shall even manage to save something to add to your settlements? I have promised to try—that is, unless Jane's wedding clothes bankrupt me.

Your loving father,
T Bennet

Elizabeth put the letter down feeling equal parts amazement and irritation. Her father was finally putting some effort into restraining her younger sisters, which was wonderful and an answer to her prayers. But to read his contemptuous words about *Mr Darcy*! It was the idea of a marriage to *Mr Collins* which should have caused his deepest distress! Elizabeth could not even imagine what it would have been like to waken from the tonic's stupor to find herself irrevocably tied to that imbecile; it was her guardian angel, in the form of Fitzwilliam Darcy, who had prevented it.

Papa's letter should be singing his praises!

Further reflection, however, gave her pause. *Am I not somewhat to blame? If I have not done as much to wound Mr Darcy's reputation as Mr Wickham, neither did I help it in any manner—blind to any of his goodness and sensitive to his every flaw, all in favour of my pride.* Beyond ensuring her family knew of his callous remarks at the assembly, she had repeated Mr Wickham's stories as if they were fact, and searched for fault in his every look or action.

It *was* good to read of Jane's new happiness, and while

she was sorry she had not been available to comfort her sister, it was just as well she had not been at home in the dark hours following Mr Bingley's departure and the letter from his sister. *Knowing my former antagonism, I probably would have blamed Mr Darcy for that, too.*

If only he would visit! Once again, she smothered the wish before it could take firmer hold. He was well rid of them all, and she must settle for the life she had once been content with, being forever grateful it was not a worse fate.

CHAPTER 11

Not a week had passed before wonderful news arrived from Longbourn: Jane was engaged to Mr Bingley. Jane's happiness overflowed in her letter, and Elizabeth was genuinely pleased for her dearest sister.

She was also envious. Mr Darcy had neither called nor left word of any kind. A tiny tentacle of hope that had refused to be crushed was finally withering its slow death. Realising he had not been forced to honourable action, he had reconsidered his options. *It is all for the best,* she told herself. According to Jane, there was not a whisper of rumour regarding her reasons for removing to town. All was well. There was time, if she met him in the future—perhaps even at Jane's wedding—to learn to pretend. She was now rehearsing the pretence every day; never mind that she expected to do so for the rest of her life. After all, once having been almost in love with Mr Darcy, who else could compare?

She and Mrs Gardiner were sitting together in the breakfast parlour on a grey winter's morning the very day after the news of Jane's engagement, when their attention was suddenly drawn to the window by the sound of a carriage—a chaise and four coming up the drive. It was too early for visitors, and besides, the equipage did not answer to that of any of their neighbours. Neither the carriage, nor the livery of the servant who preceded it, were familiar to them. As it was certain, however, that *somebody* was coming, she and her aunt went to the formal drawing room to await them.

The housekeeper soon entered. "Lady Catherine de Bourgh," she said, giving her card to Mrs Gardiner. A large, tall woman followed the presentation of the card.

"We have not been introduced," the woman announced to the room at large, her tone imperious, her every feature a demanding imprint upon a face which might once have been handsome. "I expect, however, that you know who I am."

Elizabeth recalled the name—Mr Collins's patroness, and Mr Darcy's aunt—possessing a daughter she wished him to marry.

"You are Miss Bennet?" she said, rounding upon Elizabeth.

"I am," Elizabeth replied. The uncivil air of the woman put her back up; however, she was determined, for Mr Darcy's sake, to be polite.

"And that lady is your aunt?" she asked ungraciously.

"She is. Mrs Gardiner," she added, although no introduction had been requested.

Lady Catherine proceeded, in very short order, to issue a critique on the location of the home and its placement off the street, the west-facing windows, the arrangement of the furniture, and the fabrics used in its upholstery, saying all as if she was entitled, by right of birth, to come into a stranger's home and issue disparagements.

Elizabeth glanced at Mrs Gardiner—and to her surprise, she saw that her aunt was holding back laughter. In that moment, something inside of her eased. She did not have to protect anyone here today. She would benefit from Mrs Gardiner's example, and live up to the behaviour of a *true* lady—regardless of birth—while this one made herself ridiculous.

"Since you hold such disapproval of my home," Mrs Gardiner interrupted when Lady Catherine paused for breath, "you will please forgive my surprise that you have entered it. I am certain I received no prior warning of your arrival."

Brilliant, Auntie! Elizabeth thought. Lady Catherine had never before called nor left her card—vulgar violations of basic etiquette.

Lady Catherine simply pretended not to have heard. "Miss Bennet, I require a private word with you. Does this home even possess a garden walk? I should be glad to take a turn in it, if you will favour me with your company."

But the lady had not counted on Mrs Margaret Gardiner,

who refused to be cowed by her disdain. "Unfortunately, your ladyship, I do not know you, and nothing in our very brief *un*-acquaintance leads me to believe my niece ought to be left alone in your company. If you have anything to say to her, you may say it in my hearing. Anything which I may not hear is, frankly, better left unsaid."

Lady Catherine looked down her nose with a hostile stare, and narrowed her eyes; Mrs Gardiner remained implacable and unaffected. Finally, her ladyship gave it up and proceeded, again, to pretend the other woman did not exist.

"Let us sit down. Miss Bennet, you can be at no loss to understand my reason for coming."

They sat, and Elizabeth did not hesitate in replying. "Indeed, you are mistaken. I have not been able to account for it at all."

"I have been to visit my nephew, Mr Fitzwilliam Darcy. Do you pretend to be unacquainted with him? I have heard an insupportable claim, and I demand to have it countered."

"Until I have any idea what the claim is, I can hardly contradict it."

"It is that you so deceived my nephew as to convince him of some false notion of rescue, so that instead of marrying my vicar and remaining in the sphere you were born to, you might marry him instead. He says that the marriage has not yet taken place, but he refuses to promise that it never will."

Despite Lady Catherine's disingenuous description of

the affair, it was all Elizabeth could do not to smile. "How kind of Mr Darcy. He wishes to protect my reputation."

The housekeeper entered with a tea tray, and Lady Catherine was forced to hold her tongue until the servant departed.

"The very idea is insupportable! He is engaged to my daughter!"

"Then you have nothing to worry over, do you?" Elizabeth, copying Mrs Gardiner's disinterested, unaffected air, turned instead to the tea tray. "Might I serve the tea for you, Aunt?"

Lady Catherine glared at this activity, as if they ought to remain awed in frozen silence while in her presence.

"Their engagement is of an informal nature. It was the dying wish of his mother. Are you so lost to delicacy, that you could ignore his family's claims upon him?"

Elizabeth poured her aunt's cup, adding a touch of fresh cream. "If I can ignore *your* insults, I can certainly ignore *that*. Here you are, Aunt. Biscuit?"

"Thank you, yes, Elizabeth," Mrs Gardiner said, taking a sip. "You know just how I like it."

Her ladyship's eyes narrowed. "Unfeeling, selfish girl! Do you not consider that a connexion with you must disgrace him in the eyes of everybody?"

Mrs Gardiner frowned, opening her mouth to respond, but Elizabeth gave her a little shake of her head. "I certainly do not. You are wasting your time. I am neither standing in the way of his marriage to Miss de Bourgh, nor preventing him from offering for her. If he wishes to do so, he certainly might—and, it seems to me, could have already."

It was as if she had not spoken. "You have no regard, then, for the honour and credit of my nephew?"

"It is due *to* his honour and credit that he has refused to give you the promise you demand."

"Nonsense! Mr Collins has told me of a disgusting scene—at a public inn, no less—in which you made a sordid spectacle of yourself, but I have sworn him to silence! Believe me when I say that he shall not ever mention it again—he will never dare even *think* of it! You are to understand, Miss Bennet, that I came here with the determined resolution of carrying my purpose. You have no fortune, I am told. Providentially, I am a most generous woman. You will be happy to learn that I have decided to take your impoverishment under consideration, in examining your previous conduct. Promise that you will not marry my nephew, and a thousand pounds will be yours now—the same amount, I understand, you will receive upon your mother's death. I have not been used to submit to the whims of any such a person as you. You will accept my liberality, and our association will be at an end. I have not been in the habit of brooking disappointment."

That blabbermouth Mr Collins obviously gossiped, and this shrew believes me to be a grasping, conniving, deceiver! Had Elizabeth not been determined to counter the old lady's coarseness with an opposite behaviour, she might have sunk to her level with a few sarcastic rejoinders.

"I am certain you believe yourself to be offering

protection to your nephew, but you betray your daughter's private concerns to a disinterested party. I will never speak of what occurred on the road to London. It is all to be forgot. You waste your time and mine mentioning it. It is to him that you must give your assurances, and fifty times that amount would not buy me."

"Assurances! He requires more than that, obstinate, headstrong girl! He swears he will wed you before the year is out whether Collins speaks or not! He has been confounded by your arts and allurements, and in a moment of selfish infatuation, has forgot his obligations."

"You have said more than enough," Mrs Gardiner said, standing. "I shall see you out. Perhaps you are satisfied with such unbecoming conduct as you have demonstrated in word and action this morning—but my niece is accustomed to a much higher standard of behaviour. We are finished here."

Lady Catherine's voice rose to the level of a shriek. "I am shocked and astonished. But do not deceive yourself into a belief that I will ever recede. I shall not go away till I have been given the promise I require!"

It looked very much as though, if Mrs Gardiner wished her ladyship gone, she would have to have her removed—perhaps with ropes and oxen, Elizabeth feared. But at that moment, Vincent, Mr Gardiner's man, entered without knocking. Vincent was quietly dressed and even quieter of manner. However, having been raised on the docks, he had made himself indispensable to Mr Gardiner in a hundred ways—one of which was his ability to scent trouble from two floors away.

"Shall I call for the master, Mistress?" he said in his very quiet voice.

There was something about Vincent that warned one not to cross him, and even Lady Catherine was not proof against it.

She stood, sniffed, and stalked out, Vincent stepping back to permit her exit—and probably to ensure she actually departed. But at the door, she stopped. "You do not deserve my attention. Do not suppose this matter is finished. I *will* carry my point."

Vincent closed the door behind her; Elizabeth and Mrs Gardiner stared at each other.

"Well," said her aunt. "That was something."

Elizabeth grinned, and then, because she could not help herself, laughed aloud.

Mrs Gardiner raised a brow, although she smiled back. "She was absurd, was she not? I did not mind her silly opinions of my home, but her accusations against you were insupportable. I cannot find amusement in it yet, but give me an hour or so. I am certain by the time I relay the tale to your uncle, we shall all be chuckling."

"There is little to respect about her," Elizabeth agreed, reining in her laughter. Nonetheless, she could not help the happiness bubbling through her.

Mr Darcy was a man perfectly capable of speaking his mind—and was also a man of strong opinions. It was possible that his aunt had goaded him into saying it, but the very fact of his refusal to affirm that a marriage was not imminent—never mind promising her that it *was*—told Elizabeth that his feelings remained unchanged. It was not, perhaps, the message Lady Catherine had intended to deliver, but it *was* the one received.

He *wanted* to marry her, still. She did not understand why he stayed away, but hope, like the resilient phoenix, rose up again from the ashes of her disappointment.

Exactly two weeks after Darcy and Elizabeth's adventure on the road to London, he presented himself upon the Gardiners' doorstep. He wore his finest coat, a green wool tailored by Weston, his boots polished to a nearly blinding gleam; his man—obviously sensing romance in the air—had fussed over his cravat endlessly. He felt like a dashed fop, even clutching a posy in the hopes of catching the eye of his lady-love while sporting an over-elaborate, dandified neckcloth.

Those nerves faded the moment he set eyes upon Elizabeth. She was dressed charmingly in yellow, her dark eyes shining, her perfect, pretty mouth smiling. For a moment he was utterly dumbfounded as feelings of adoration rushed through him, urging him to his knee right there in the parlour while her aunt looked on. He only just managed to contain them.

"Mr Darcy," Elizabeth murmured, in response to his

bowed greeting. "How lovely to see you again." She glanced at the flowers. "Are those for me?"

The sound of her voice sent a thrill through his very being. "Yes," he said, thrusting them at her like a green lad and then feeling equal parts foolish and lustful as she twinkled up at him from amongst the blossoms.

Mrs Gardiner, whom he had hardly noticed upon bringing Elizabeth to Gracechurch Street, greeted him graciously, took the flowers from Elizabeth, and made some excuse about putting them in water. Unbelievably, within minutes of his arrival, he was alone with the woman he loved.

"My aunt says you require fifty thousand to marry me," he said.

"Did she?" Elizabeth raised a brow. "And how did you respond?"

"I told her I would write the bank draft at once, if I thought you would take it—but as you are worth a hundred times the amount, I did not believe I could get you so cheaply."

She grinned, and warmth flooded him.

"Such a *reasonable* answer to give. Although I suppose it did not please your aunt."

"I could not care a farthing for her opinions." He could wait no longer, and foolish and gauche or not, he dropped to one knee. "Elizabeth, my love, keeping away from you to assure that your hand would not be forced has made for the longest two weeks of my life. Please say you will marry me, and that this is the last separation we must ever endure."

To his surprise, she, too, went down on her knees before him. "I am not nearly so honourable as you," she said, wrapping her arms around him. "I shall endanger your reputation, thoroughly, so that you shall have to marry me immediately." She moved her lips to his.

She was far too innocent to know exactly what her words meant, he realised, and happily returned her kiss; what she lacked in experience, she made up for in enthusiasm and he quickly realised he could be carried away, right here in her aunt's parlour unless he allowed his better self to govern *at once*. Carefully he stood, drawing her up with him, struggling to contain his own passion.

"I missed you," she murmured against his lips, and his heart swelled.

"I shall get a licence," he said.

"I shall write to Papa today. He can give any permission necessary." She bit her lip, looking up at him with a little hesitation. "Did you know that Mr Bingley is returned to Netherfield? He has evidently asked for Jane's hand."

"I knew. I was not certain your sister wished to give her hand to Bingley, but I told him that she is a woman of integrity and he must be very certain of her feelings before pressing." He smiled. "I did hope he would press, however. I was devious, you see. I thought perhaps if your sister became attached to my good friend, you might think better of my own suit."

She smiled back. “I do like how you think, Mr Darcy. However, Jane’s feelings for Mr Bingley have never been in doubt. Cannot you tell a woman in love when you see one?”

He brushed her cheek with one hand. “I am afraid to hope. We did not begin—*I* did not begin well.”

“It is fortunate, then, that we are to be given more than one beginning,” she replied softly.

EPILOGUE

It was a wedding breakfast to end all wedding breakfasts.

"Mama has outdone herself," Elizabeth whispered. Her husband smiled. He truly followed a gentleman's code, and when it came to her mother, he usually had very little to say. He watched Mrs Bennet like a hawk, however, not trusting her judgment, let alone her table. He had sworn that he would taste every dish before Elizabeth was allowed to consume it, for the rest of her mother's natural life.

"She will never do such a thing again," she murmured, as he cut a small sliver off her honey cake.

"She will not, lest she be put on the next sailing bound for New South Wales," he murmured back. Yet, he ate the bite anyway and nodded his approval. "I do it so she *knows* I am always watching her. I never want her to be too comfortable around me, so that you may be always comfortable around her."

Elizabeth smiled, and under the table, well-hidden by the tablecloth, squeezed his knee. Because she could—and never tired of teasing him, she moved her hand a bit higher.

"Careful, my girl," he warned. "However safe you think yourself from your mother, there are other dangers in the room."

"I am not afraid of you," she grinned.

Her husband did not return her smile, but only draped a casual arm over the back of her chair.

"How much longer is the performance?" he leant close to ask.

Elizabeth glanced around. Her mother had actually knocked down a wall between the dining room and the breakfast parlour in order to create one huge dining hall, complete with a dais at one end upon which she had arranged the seating for her most illustrious guests. It really did appear as though she and Darcy were on a stage.

"They will just have the toasts now," she whispered back. "If everyone is as brief as my father's will be, not long."

But it was Bingley who stood, rather than Mr Bennet, tapping his crystal flute with an attention-getting chime.

"Welcome, everyone! Welcome! How happy I have been to see you all! How delighted my family is to share this wonderful day with so many of our friends!"

"Oh, perfect, your mother has enlisted the lengthiest toast-maker in the kingdom," Darcy muttered drily.

"Whatever shall we do to pass the time?" she teased, her hand a featherweight touch upon him beneath the tablecloth.

Something within those dark eyes of his flared, and she felt her husband's thumb graze the bare skin at her nape, an almost imperceptible motion of his hand, causing gooseflesh to rise.

"Firstly, to our host and hostess, Mr and Mrs Bennet, at whose fine, heavily laden tables today we gather to celebrate the marriage of their daughter and new son, lift your glass in a toast!"

The crowd dutifully raised their glasses to her mother and father; Mr Bennet appeared quite satisfied—as well he might be with such a son to join his family—and Mrs Bennet beamed. Elizabeth would never truly understand the relationship between her parents, but she did know that they had somehow bridged many of their differences ever since her mother's noxious interference in her life. *At least Papa has taken more seriously his duties as a father, while Mama pays him a good deal of attention—and I will not think any further on* that *than I have to! However one considers it, his health has been exceptional ever since.*

"Secondly, a toast to Miss Mary for the brilliant playing we heard today," Bingley continued. "Her mastery of the church's pipe organ provides music that is a gift to us all. Hear, hear!"

He lifted his glass, and Elizabeth was pleased to see

her neighbours join him with cheering enthusiasm for her sister's talent, with her uncle Gardiner leaning over to kiss her sister's cheek and her aunt nodding appreciatively. It was Darcy who had hired Mary a master for the complicated instrument, with its multiple keyboards and soaring pipes—and also who had had the magnificent organ installed in Meryton's church.

"Thank you for helping her," she leant over to him to whisper.

He shrugged. "Look at her face," he said simply. Elizabeth glanced over at Mary, whose cheeks were pink with delight, her smile wide—she looked almost beautiful in the pleasure of her hard-earned recognition.

Bingley's voice interrupted the merry congratulations of her neighbours. "And speaking of the church—although I am certain the beloved Mr Palmer is much missed—we can all take heart in the fine services conducted by Mr Ludlow. Never were any bride and groom better ushered into holy wedlock. Mrs Ludlow, may I mention that I have never seen the church so exquisitely bedecked in blossoms? I fear you denuded the rectory garden in support of your sister's wedding, a gift of beauty on this happy day." He raised his glass towards Kitty and her husband, the village's new vicar, who both smiled happily as the room cheered. The former Charlotte Lucas, wed to Pemberley's vicar, Mr Bradley—and thus an expert in village weddings—had come home from Derbyshire to visit on this great occasion, and leant over and whispered some obvious compliment, for Kitty's smile showed even brighter.

"If Bingley begins an admiration of the church's plasterwork and stained-glass windows, I shall toss my glass at *him,*" Darcy muttered, so that only she could hear. He had a certain gift, a way of both touch and whisper, that caused her awareness of him to climb sharply up her spine and through her every nerve. He followed it by a look, a look that revealed to her—and only her—a naked wanting, quickly shuttered before the crowded dining hall could notice.

"I cannot toast anyone else until I have raised my glass to my own beloved wife," Bingley proclaimed, beginning a recital of Jane's many perfections.

"Dear lord," Darcy murmured. "It appears he means to keep us here for the rest of the summer."

She grinned at him. "I can think of many worse places to be."

"A challenge, my dear?" he replied, and then set about driving her mad.

He knew just how to do it, of course. The brief touches, his whispered approvals of everything from the colour of her gown to the arrangement of her hair, and how pleased he would be when they were alone again and he would be free to touch and do and say all of what he felt for her. Elizabeth slowly fanned herself, trying to pay attention to the endless toast and not betray her weakness for the man beside her…*the wretch.*

"Let us see," Bingley said, pinching his chin thoughtfully. "Have I forgotten anyone?"

Lydia giggled.

"Ah, yes, Mr and Mrs Darcy. What can I say of two people who are known far and wide as one of the most ravishing couples in the kingdom? The *ton* is still whispering about the number of times you required Mr John Bridge, of the renowned jewellers Rundell, Bridge, and Rundell, to cart ever-greater trays of astonishing stones to Mayfair—in the hopes of winning your approval for a stone fine enough to celebrate your engagement. Was it three times or four that you sent him tottering in defeat back to Ludgate Hill?"

"It was only twice—I quickly discovered that no stone on earth would truly be fine enough for my bride," Darcy drawled. "The Pigot Diamond was still in France at the time, you understand, forcing me to settle for something less, hm, substantial."

The crowd's attention was drawn, quite naturally, to the exquisite ring of sizeable diamonds and sapphires upon Elizabeth's finger, which happened, at that very moment, to capture the morning light in a blinding flash —generating a great deal of good-hearted laughter.

"We thank you all for coming to Longbourn, for celebrating this happiest of occasions with us, for being our friends and our family. One more toast: Champagne to our real friends and real pain to our sham ones!" Bingley raised his glass.

Almost as one, the gathering cheered, and Bingley made a show of retaking his seat.

"Mr Bingley! You forgot us!" Lydia exclaimed.

"What? Oh, dear me! I seem to have neglected to toast the bride and bridegroom!"

"Would that she let it go," Darcy murmured.

"She has been planning this wedding with Mama for, oh, twenty-four of her twenty-five years now. She must have her moment in the sun." She gave her husband a sideways glance. "Besides, 'tis you who encouraged your friend Mr Montclair to take Netherfield in the first place, and you who introduced him to Lydia. One might say this lengthy proceeding is all your fault."

He shrugged. "He was too inclined to dullness, and requires a lively bride. I had to wait for her to achieve a modicum of restraint before introductions could be made, however, which took longer than I supposed."

Elizabeth shook her head, smiling. He did not fool her for a minute—her interfering husband had been unable to rest until each of her sisters were happy or happily settled. Ten years of marriage had taught her that he was the very best of men. She leant over to whisper in his ear. "I love you."

Bingley finished his speech at that moment, to great applause and clinking glasses. The moment the guests began converging on the head table, Darcy whisked her away, out the door, down the private paths they knew so well from their previous visits, towards the lovely cottage he'd had constructed out of sight of the main house—closer to Meryton on land adjoining, that *he* had purchased, and not a part of the estate. Someday, once her father was gone, it would be home to her mother and

Mary, that they might not ever have to share one with Mr Collins—who had, as yet, never convinced *anyone* to marry him. Her husband's generosity truly knew no bounds.

"In such a hurry?" she teased again, once they reached the cottage door. But instead of entering, he leant against it, grinning down at her, his hands placed rather tantalisingly upon her shoulders.

"Inside this home," he said, "I have no doubt, the Harwoods will have prepared us a quiet, private meal of our own." His trustworthy valet had retired from his illustrious career as a gentleman's gentleman and accepted a generous pension—both Mr and Mrs Darcy were deeply indebted to him and never forgot it. To their surprise, he returned to Hertfordshire and promptly married the former Mrs Hill. Together, the couple had embarked upon a second career, becoming the cottage's caretakers.

"Inside this home," he repeated, "is a lovely suite of rooms, furnished to my wife's tasteful particulars, which happens to include a soft, rather splendid bed. I will tell you what is *not* within this home: three obstinate, headstrong children who have a terrible habit of popping up in all the places one would rather *not* see them."

Elizabeth Darcy smiled up at him. "Perhaps, if they did not have such an affectionate father, whose pockets were not often full of sweets and other surprises, they might grant him more of that privacy he desires."

His expression grew serious. "What I desire most," he said softly, "is the wife of my heart, bare in the morning light, so that I might show her all the ways I am still in love with her—a thousand times more today than a decade ago. Will you come with me, my darling?"

"Always," she whispered.

He lifted her in his strong arms, carrying her over the threshold to a new and glorious celebration of their very own.

The End

ALSO BY JULIE COOPER

A Match Made at Matlock

A Stronger Impulse

A Yuletide Dream

Irresistibly Alone

Lost and Found

Nameless

Seek Me: Georgiana's Story

Tempt Me

The Bachelor Mr Darcy

The Perfect Gentleman

The Seven Sins of Fitzwilliam Darcy

Multi-Author Projects

'Tis the Season

A Match Made at Matlock

Happily Ever After with Mr Darcy

ABOUT THE AUTHOR

Julie Cooper lives with her husband of forty-one years in Central California. She spends her time boasting of her four brilliant and beautiful children, doting on her four brilliant and beautiful grandchildren, and cleaning up after her neurotic Bichon, Pogo. Somewhere in between the truly important stuff, she peddles fruit baskets and chocolate-covered strawberries for a living whilst pressing penitent Mr Darcys on an unsuspecting public.

ACKNOWLEDGMENTS

Many thanks are due to Amy D'Orazio and Jan Ashton of Quills & Quartos Publishing for editing this work.

Printed in Great Britain
by Amazon

47833298R00088